THE
ACCIDENTAL
WIZARD

A
PECULIAR
PROBLEM

For Max, my partner in crime,
and Tony, for 25 years (and still counting!)

Published in the UK by Scholastic, 2022
Euston House, 24 Eversholt Street, London, NW1 1DB
Scholastic Ireland, 89E Lagan Road, Dublin Industrial Estate,
Glasnevin, Dublin, D11 HP5F

SCHOLASTIC and associated logos are trademarks
and/or registered trademarks of Scholastic Inc.

Text © Kimberly Pauley, 2022
Illustrations © Robin Boyden, 2022

The right of Kimberly Pauley and Robin Boyden to be identified
as the author and illustrator of this work has been asserted
by them under the Copyright, Designs and Patents Act 1988.

ISBN 978 1407 19572 8

A CIP catalogue record for this book is available
from the British Library.

Printed by CPI Group (UK) Ltd, Croydon, CR0 4YY
Paper made from wood grown in sustainable forests
and other controlled sources.

1 3 5 7 9 10 8 6 4 2

www.scholastic.co.uk

THE ACCIDENTAL WIZARD

A PECULIAR PROBLEM

KIMBERLY PAULEY

ILLUSTRATED BY ROBIN BOYDEN

SCHOLASTIC

THE
KINGDOMS

BONE END

KNEECAP

KRAKEN'S TOOTHPICK

THE MOANING CAVES

SHIP'S GRAVEYARD

N
NW *NE*
W *E*
SW *SE*
S

THE EYE
OF THE SEA

IN WHICH THINGS TAKE ROOT

"Pixie *Pooooosssssstttttt!*"

The high-pitched voice of the delivery pixie oozed sparkles and fairy dust. Twig Thicket groaned and clamped his pillow – which rather horribly smelled like unwashed gnome – down over his head.

It didn't help. *"De-livery* for Twig Thicket, wizard *extra-or-dinaire!"* Zinnia Coreopsis Borage was a pixie who never spoke when she could trill.

"Not so loud," Twig said, his voice muffled.

"Post *away*! You're *welcome!"* Two rather heavy somethings thudded on to the pillow on top of his head. He sighed and sat up, looking around the small

1

tent-like enclosure he'd magicked up the night before out of some shrubs and small trees. It was all he'd had to work with in this scrubby north-western edge of the Eternal Forest. He'd even made sure to close the makeshift tent up tight with all the thorny bits sticking out, but Zinnia always managed to find a way in, no matter what precautions he took. Pixies were like that. Persistent.

"I hate pixies, *especially* that one," said Vile, who had rolled herself up in her blanket in a corner. All Twig could see of her was a mass of red hair coming out the top. He had learned over the last few moons that hags were definitely not morning people.

"Ye hate everyone," said Glimfinkle,

who was also not his very best in the mornings. Or afternoons. The gnome had made his bed in their sadly very empty money pouch. It hung from a small branch in the middle of the tent because Twig had learned that the gnome's snoring was slightly more tolerable from above. At the moment, only his head stuck out, his hat on backwards.

"One more *mess-age*! For Twig Thicket, wizard *extra-or-dinaire*!" Zinnia twisted around once in the air and somehow managed to make herself look heavy-shouldered and blocky. She took a deep breath, giving Twig just enough time to brace himself.

"TWIG THICKET! DO YOU MEAN TO TELL ME YOU'VE ALREADY SPENT ALL YOUR PRIZE MONEY AND HAVE NOTHING LEFT TO SEND TO YOUR POOR OLD MUM?! WHY DON'T YOU COME BACK TO MUCKWOOD AND WORK FOR THE KING LIKE I TOLD YOU TO? WHERE ARE YOU? THAT MISERABLE OLD WIZARD RIPPLEMINTZ WON'T TELL ME. DON'T YOU KNOW THAT—"

Zinnia stopped to take another breath. Twig hastily stuffed a sugar cube right in her mouth before she could finish his mum's message. He didn't really want to know what else Nettle Thicket had said. It was always the same thing – come back home to Muckwood. Adventuring was best left to older, wiser, *better* people.

"Consider the rest of the message delivered," Twig told the pixie.

"Suit yourself," said Zinnia, barely able to speak around the sugar cube. Then came the familiar *POP!* as she whisked away back to the small kingdom of Muckwood, leagues and a lifetime away on the other side of the Eternal Forest.

"What did ye get this time, Twig? Anything nice and shiny and gold?" Glimfinkle scratched his beard, tangling it up even worse. Vile had a permanent case of bedhead, but Glimfinkle had started to develop bedbeard as a consequence of months of camping out.

Twig looked around for what was new among their meagre belongings and found a small green velvet pouch intricately decorated with an embroidered floral pattern. He tossed it in Vile's general direction. She grunted when it landed on her stomach. "Why

4

don't you look after this one? It must be from Witch Wormwood. It certainly isn't from my mum. Probably more dragon mint."

Witch Wormwood was quite nice, as witches went, and had given him lots of somewhat useful advice since he had met her, but now that she was back home in the Withering Swamp and he was out adventuring, she mostly just kept him in good supply of treats. His mum, on the other hand, never sent anything good. She didn't understand that there were really only two ways to learn how to be a great wizard: apprentice with a master (which Ripplemintz, his old mentor, was definitely *not*) or learn by doing – which meant travelling the kingdoms, given his unique situation. By winning the wizard's duel at the Euphonium, the yearly competition for magic users and spellcasters from across the kingdoms he'd guaranteed that no other kingdom's head wizard wanted to take him on as an apprentice, not when they thought he was after their job. Even Ripplemintz didn't want him back, though he'd never say so.

"Anythin' else? Mebbe somethin' shiny?" The

gnome sounded hopeful, though Twig had no idea who Glimfinkle thought would be *sending* Twig gold. Usually it was the Thicket family asking him for some.

"Oh," said Twig, picking up some rolled-up papers from where they were half-buried in his blanket, "looks like the latest *Wizard Quarterly*."

Vile had managed to unfurl herself. She snatched the magazine out of his hand, straightened it out, took one look, and then waved it gleefully in his face. "And look who's on the cover!"

Twig grabbed it back. It was an image of him from the award ceremony at the Euphonium. A beaming wizard, Salamar, was handing him the prize bag of gold for winning the wizard duel and a commemorative statuette of Marsh Griddle, the very first winner of the Euphonium one hundred years before.

Twig squinted. It certainly wasn't the best picture of him. He looked somewhere in the middle of confused and exhausted, and his mouth was wide open like a fish. Though, to be fair, he *had* been both confused and exhausted at the time.

Vile took it back. "Oi!" she said, with a barely

contained snort. "Did you read what it says underneath? Twig Thicket, winner of the 100th Annual Euphonium. Voted *Wizard Quarterly*'s Stupidest Wizard of the Year."

"Lookit that," said Glimfinkle solemnly, mostly managing to hold back a laugh. "Yer famous, ye are."

Wizard Quarterly

Twig Thicket, Youngest Winner Ever at the 100th Annual Euphonium!

Wizard Root

Voted *Wizard Quarterly's* Stupidest Wizard of the Year

This year's Euphonium was full of surprises, and most of them centred around the upstart newcomer wizard Twig Thicket of Muckwood. Not only did he survive a casting of Nix's Unravelling during a duel with Bragmore's Sumac Crabapple, he went on to handily win the entire competition. He defeated Kudzu of the Spire in record time. So, how, you ask, does that earn him *Wizard Quarterly's* Stupidest Wizard of the Year honour? Simple, my erudite friends: by willingly GIVING AWAY his power to Kudzu during the duel! This wizard is sure it was sheer surprise that knocked Kudzu off the mound. *[more on page 12]*

Vile Hornwort Defeats Older Sister to Win Hag Scrap

Phlox Pigeontoe

The Hornworts have always been the ones to watch in a hag scrap, and this year's Euphonium event was no exception. After flattening the field with a flurry of boils, cantankerous sores and even trench toe, it was sister against sister. It was anyone's hag scrap until the younger sister pulled out all the stops and cast a stunning variation of the Rapunzel curse on her sister Nasty: voted last year's Haggiest Hag, Nasturtium Hornwort now stands toe to toe with the prettiest of princesses.

[more on page 13]

Twig tried to grab the *Wizard Quarterly* from Vile, but she leapfrogged around the small space, keeping it out of his reach, all while reading out from the article. It wasn't very complimentary at all, even if he *had* won the grand prize. The bit about *her* winning the hag scrap competition was much nicer. It wasn't fair.

"Interestin' colour ye've turned there," said Glimfinkle. "Whaddaya call that?"

"Beetroot?" Vile was still snort-giggling. She finally finished reading the front page out and tossed the magazine back to him. He snatched it up and stuffed it in his pack.

"Shut up," said Twig, gathering the rest of his things and jamming them in his bag. "Both of you."

"At least they wrote about you. They didn't even mention me," grumped Glimfinkle, shimmying out of the money pouch and jumping down to the ground.

"Why would they? *You* didn't win any grand prizes like we did," said Vile.

"Not like ye could've done it without me!"

This was an old argument now. "Glimfinkle, put a sock in it. Can't we please just pack up and get on with it?" Twig waved his hands and muttered the spell that put the trees and bushes back to where they were supposed to be. The morning air was crisp and a bit chilly as it rushed in.

"Oh, don't get me started on ye!" yelled Glimfinkle, glaring at Twig. "Yer supposed to be the world's greatest wizard and what's that got us?" He stomped around in a circle, kicking acorns out of his way. "It's only been three full moons since you won the Euphonium and we're out of gold and livin' in a bloomin' glorified tent!"

Twig couldn't argue with that even if he had the energy to. The gnome was right. Everything had seemed all bright and shiny after he'd won the wizard duel at the 100th Annual Euphonium. There'd been congratulations from every witch, wizard, hag and peasant around. And since he'd won by very spectacularly giving away some of his magic power to the wizard Kudzu of the Spire, he'd even managed to get out from under the finger of the king of Muckwood, since the king had thought Twig had given away *all* of his power and so decided not to bother with him. It had seemed like a clever idea at the time. Then Twig's mum had let it slip to the king that Twig still had magic, and now he couldn't go home unless he took over as the official wizard of Muckwood.

Besides not wanting to take away Ripplemintz's position, he didn't feel at all experienced enough to be the official wizard of anywhere. He didn't much like King Mervyn either. He'd once seen him order someone's *hands* to be chopped off for stealing. Not that thieving was good, but still. Twig had been hungry before. Desperate people sometimes did desperate things. In fact, he was pretty well famished all the time lately. Just not quite starving enough to go back to Muckwood without having learned anything yet.

"Well," said Vile, kicking an acorn back at Glimfinkle, "and whose magpie has been eating us out of house and home? All the gold's gone to feeding Beaky!"

There was a bellowing screech from the tree up above them and they all instinctively ducked.

"Not my fault," said Glimfinkle, much more quietly, and with a furtive glance up. "Who's the one who turned my sweet little magpie into a bloomin' boobrie?" He and Vile both turned to glare at Twig.

"I offered to change him back," said Twig lamely. "But you said yourself that he didn't want to be normal again." And it definitely wasn't prudent to argue with Beaky now that he was mostly boobrie, a *very* large magical flying creature that could probably swallow them whole without blinking an eye.

The former magpie was quite pleased with being a part-time boobrie. On the plus side, they could all ride him when he was big and get to places super fast. And absolutely nothing bothered them when Beaky was around in his boobrie form, since boobrie were so massive that they regularly ate cows. They hadn't even had any ogre trouble. Ogres preferred eating people to being eaten.

On the downside, Beaky had to consume an enormous amount of food to maintain his size, and if he didn't get enough, he shrank back down to his normal magpie self. This was terribly unfortunate if it happened while they were in the middle of a flight, which they'd found out the hard way the first time they'd ridden him. Crash landings hurt.

Twig sighed. They'd been having this same argument, or some variation of it, for the last couple of weeks. He didn't know what to do about it. It was tiring.

"You know," he said, for probably the hundredth time, "if it's as bad as all that, you don't have to go adventuring with me. The two of you are safe to go back to Muckwood any time you want."

Vile snorted. "Go back to that titchy little hag hut that stunk of troll? Anything's a palace compared to that."

Glimfinkle threw an acorn at Twig. "A pox on ye fer sayin' such a thing! Ye know I'm a gnome wot's too big for a place like Muckwood. We've got grand things in front of us, I just knows it!"

"Stop feeling sorry for yourself, Twig," said Vile. "We've got bigger fish to fry. We *have* to go shopping today for certain or you'll have to come up with a good spell to make chokecherry berries into something edible. That's all I've found around here."

Twig had yet to find a spell that would do anything to make chokecherry berries taste good. And it wasn't just the taste – it was the after-effects too. Even his mum's acorn stew was better.

"Fallow's closest," said Glimfinkle. "Hour or so walk, or mebbe five minutes on Beaky." Hearing his name again, Beaky flew down and landed in front of them in a flurry of black feathers.

"Beaky it is," said Twig. There *were* definite benefits to having him around.

They hopped aboard the boobrie, Twig in front and Vile behind, with Glimfinkle tucked away in a small leather harness around Beaky's neck.

They had barely gone up when Beaky began to descend again. He landed on one side of Fallow, behind a tumbledown barn that looked abandoned. There was a small overgrown orchard but not much else.

Fallow was so small that it could barely be called a village. It was on the northernmost edge of the Eternal Forest, an area known for spindly trees and poor dirt. Not much that was edible or useful grew around the area, which was one reason the last few weeks had been very hungry ones. Between nothing to forage and folks too poor to hire them, it had been very lean pickings.

Twig had never even heard of Fallow before, but that wasn't unusual. Until he'd accidentally become the world's greatest wizard, he'd never really left Muckwood. Now here he was clear on the other side of the Eternal Forest, which he'd always thought would be a lot bigger than it was, given the name.

They left Beaky behind the barn with the last of their bread and the crumbly remains of a mincemeat pie that Twig had traded an unbreakable plough spell for. It was still early in the morning and the streets were quiet. They split up, Vile going one way and Twig and Glimfinkle the other, and met back in the middle. They'd walked the entire length of the village in only ten minutes and met with just three people, only one of whom had nodded a begrudging hello. Vile reported one pub and a herbalist. Twig had found a couple of shuttered storefronts and a blacksmith. Glimfinkle pointed out a Pixie Post box, but even that looked small and ill-kept, and none of them were in the mood to send any mail ... or talk to a pixie. Fallow didn't look very promising as far as finding work went. Or decent food. The pub had been called the Lame Goat.

Vile pulled out the pouch delivered earlier. "Well, maybe Witch Wormwood sent some food. At this point, I'd even go for one of her toadstool pies." She pulled on the string that held the pouch closed and went to peek inside.

But as soon as she opened it, a gush of flowers and vines began pouring out like a river of green dotted about with splashes of blue and yellow and crimson.

"Gah!" was all she managed to say before a particularly hardy grapevine sprang forth, bloomed, and then popped out with bunches of ripe fruit and buried her in clusters of purple grapes. Twig lost sight of her almost immediately, but that could have been because he was busy fighting off something sticky with lots of tiny white flowers that grew so fast it was halfway up his body before he'd even managed to figure out what was happening.

2

IN WHICH THERE IS A SMALL BLOOM OF HOPE

Twig batted at the sticky plant, but only managed to cover his arms in the stuff. Glimfinkle, clinging desperately to Twig's ear, had a few choice words to say. "Stop playin' with the flowers and jus' make it stop, ye silly wizard!"

"Right," said Twig. "Sorry ... um ... *grow no more!*" It didn't rhyme, but it was all he could think of. The flow of new plants slowed to a trickle and then finally stopped completely, but he could feel the reluctance of the spell to end. It had a lot of power behind it. Very familiar-feeling power. It felt like sunshine and flowers

and lazy afternoons. He knew immediately who had
sent the spell, and it wasn't Witch Wormwood.

A dark green vine, as thick around as Twig's wrist,
had been the last thing to grow from the pouch. As
Twig's spell hit it, it stopped growing and sprouted a
scroll. The greenish parchment unfurled right in front
of Twig's face with a little pop of confetti made from
flower petals, pollen and bits of grass. He sneezed.

Greetings, young Wizard Twig!
I hope my missive finds you
well and brightens your day.
My "beauty bombs" will
certainly enhance whatever
drab environs you find yourself
in! I am planning to send
them to all my friends.
I wish to once again
convey my deepest
thanks for your
unexpected gift.
I have found the

additional power quite refreshing and am determined
to make the world a better place, thanks to you. I
invite you to visit the Spire any time you wish. You
are always welcome. I hope you visit soon, as the
beauty of the Spire is beyond compare.

Yours faithfully,

Wizard Kudzu of the Spire

Glimfinkle, still clinging on to Twig's shoulder, read the letter along with him and let out a gnomish curse. "See! Wot did I tell ye! Them half-elves ain't like people. They ain't right in the head! Ye never should've given yer power away to someone like him!"

"Um ... I'm sure he meant well," said Twig, surveying the scene. The overflow of greenery extended almost halfway through Fallow and completely filled the street around them, growing up and through the wheels of a nearby wagon and all the way over the roof of the closest house. All you could see of the Pixie Post box was the tiny chimney, still smoking, though Twig could hear the muffled shouts of a grouchy pixie even through the cover. How far would it have gone if he hadn't stopped it?

People were coming out of their houses and the pub, and some were pointing in their direction, which made sense since they were in the centre of the explosion of green. He had to admit that Fallow *looked* a lot prettier, but he strongly suspected that the villagers would not agree that it was better.

"A little help here!" Vile's voice sounded far away. Twig waded through some shrubbery and began pulling bunches of grapes out of the way, shoving them in his sack as he went. He had the feeling they might be having lunch on the run. Some of the villagers were slowly making their way towards them. One even had a pitchfork.

Vile's hand broke through, her fingers stained purple with grape juice. Twig grabbed it and hauled her out.

"What *was* that?" she asked, brushing herself off. "Did you do that?"

"It wasn't me!" said Twig, rather loudly, hoping that the villagers would hear him. They didn't look happy, especially the guy with the pitchfork. He was inspecting the overgrown wagon.

"Hey, you, kid! You a wizard?" That was from a man peering through the vines covering his windows. The door of his house was completely overwhelmed. He wouldn't be getting out without some help.

"It was that daft wizard Kudzu wot Twig gave his power to," said Glimfinkle, not even noticing the small crowd that was picking their way towards them. He gave Twig's ear a tweak. "So, yeah, it's still yer fault so far as I can tell."

"*Shhhh!*" Twig plucked the gnome from his shoulder and poked him down into the chest pocket on his travelling tunic that he'd added for that very purpose. You never knew when you might need to run from something in the Eternal Forest, like an ogre or, apparently, a mob of annoyed villagers. A few more people had appeared. Did they shovel a lot of hay in Fallow? Why did they have so many pitchforks?

"What're ye doing?" asked Glimfinkle. "I was fine where I was."

Vile had noticed the crowd too. She looked at Twig. He looked at her.

"My hag sense says it's time to run," she said.

Twig didn't bother agreeing. He just took her hand and ran.

Beaky was still where they had left him behind the barn. Luckily, none of Kudzu's handiwork had made it that far. Unluckily, he'd finished all of the food they had left him and had started eating the apples off a tree in the small orchard. This wouldn't have been so bad, but the farm wasn't as abandoned as they had thought, and the farmer was there trying to shoo Beaky away. It wasn't going well, though Twig had to give it to the man for being either very brave or very, very foolish.

Glimfinkle had finally figured out that danger was imminent. He let out a shrill whistle and Beaky stopped trying to peck the farmer's head. He flew down out of the tree and landed in front of them. They hopped aboard without slowing down, Twig grabbing a tight hold of the boobrie's neck. Vile clung like a barnacle on to his back.

"Stop, thief!" yelled the farmer.

"Get back here!" came another voice. It was pitchfork man, rounding the corner of the barn at full tilt.

"Sorry!" called Twig, as Beaky launched into the air. The bird knew a getaway when he saw one.

Three flaps and they were high above Fallow. Beaky stretched his wings and took off as fast as he could, which, all things said, was pretty quick.

"Er, Twig," yelled Vile into his ear, "Beaky's feeling a bit smallish, don't you think?"

It was true. Beaky had been close to full size the night before, but what little he'd eaten in the morning had obviously not been enough. He was only middling big now, and that wouldn't last long, not at the speed he was going and while carrying them all.

But now seemed like a very bad time to land. Fallow was on the edge of the Eternal Forest and the plains of Aramore. If they landed on the flat plains, it would be very easy to find them. If they crashed over the forest ... well, they'd done that before and it hadn't been at all pleasant. They needed to get further away from Fallow.

Twig reached into his sack that he'd slung around his neck and pulled out a bunch of grapes. "Beaky, catch!" He pitched the fruit out in front of them, hoping that Beaky would understand.

Beaky flew directly into the bunch and Twig wound up with the grapes going SPLAT into his face. Beaky let out a bellow.

"Try again, lad, but put some arm in it," said Glimfinkle, holding tight to the edge of Twig's pocket.

Twig flung another bunch into the air as hard as he could throw. Beaky managed to grab them and gobble the grapes in one gulp. Twig threw another and another, the boobrie swooping and darting to catch them. It was working. Beaky wasn't growing any larger, but at least he wasn't shrinking. Twig was feeling a bit seasick, but that was better than crashing any day.

Twig ran out of grapes around the same time they ran out of trees. All they could do now was wait and see.

"Ye can do it, ye glorious feathered beast!" Glimfinkle was as far out of Twig's pocket as he could get while still being safe. His beard fluttered and flapped in the wind. Beaky flew faster.

Ahead of them, Twig could see a river winding to the west. The Endless River. It ran from where the mermaids dwelled in the Hidden Cove, which wasn't really hidden as everyone knew where it was so they could avoid it, and then down through the plains, and marked the edge of the Eternal Forest before it split into the Witch Fingers and emptied out into the Salt Flats and, perhaps, all the way down underground to the Eye of the Sea.

"Yo, gnome, tell him to cross the river," yelled Vile. "The closest bridge is near Round Lake, so if anyone is trying to follow us, they'll be stuck on the other side of the river."

"Good thinkin'," said Glimfinkle, sounding surprised. He whistled and chirped to Beaky, who sped up a little more. The boobrie began to descend as they approached the bank of the river. He flew low across the water and even managed to scoop up a very surprised fish along the way.

Twig wasn't sure if it was his imagination or if Beaky was shrinking again, but he didn't want to take any chances. "Tell him to land behind that hill," he told Glimfinkle. Now that they were out of the plains and across the river, there were some low rolling hills.

Beaky took them in for a relatively safe landing, considering he was juggling a very large fish. There wasn't much around, just some scrub bushes and tall grass. They dismounted and looked at each other.

Twig and Vile were both covered in sticky grape juice. Vile's dress had new and interesting splotches, though only someone familiar with her style would even notice the new versus the old. Glimfinkle's beard was so windblown he looked like he was still flying at great speed. It had only been about an hour since they had broken camp. Another dismal start to another rotten day.

"I'm starvin'," said Glimfinkle. "Mebbe we could make a fire and cook up that fish—" He took a look at Beaky, who had half swallowed the fish in question already. "Eh, never mind," said the gnome.

Twig sighed. They'd have to go somewhere with food. He could use magic to make things into something, but you had to have something to start with. You couldn't make something out of nothing. And right now they were in a big bunch of nothing.

At least they could be clean.

"Let's not make a scene,

Please make us clean."

A shower of sparkles descended on them, tingling, and swept away all the accumulated dirt and stickiness. Even Glimfinkle's beard and Vile's hair were straightened up like a comb had gone over them. The hag shook her head in disgust and messed her hair up again with her fingers.

"You know I hate it when you do that," she said.

"It's better than being sticky and purple," said Twig. He sighed again. He knew she'd somehow manage to pick up a layer of twigs and leaves soon enough. It was her special talent. That, and cursing people with boils or turning them into chickens.

He took a good look around. They really were in the middle of not much. He didn't think he could make anything edible out of the tall grass around them. They weren't cows.

"So, where do we go from here? We're really out of food now and we need a job."

"How about Rockpool?" asked Vile. "It's the closest kingdom."

"Shouldn't we stick to small places because of ... *you know*." Twig tilted his head in Beaky's direction. All that was left of the fish was a tiny bit of fin stuck in his beak.

Vile pulled a crumpled parchment out of her pocket. "Yeah, but we need an actual paying job, right? We haven't found a decent gig anywhere small in ages. I think we need to think bigger." She gave the paper to Twig and he smoothed it out so he could read it. "I

snitched that from the Lame Goat before everything
went pear-shaped."

Adventurers Wanted!

*Calling all Knights, Wizards, Reformed
Highwaymen and the like.*

*Wanted: any information leading to the
return of beloved Crown Prince Igneous,
last seen headed towards the Seven Sisters
in search of a Damsel in Distress.*

Please report to Coquina Castle, Rockpool.

"Reward definitely sounds right promising," said
Glimfinkle, rubbing his little hands together. "I like the
sound of that, I do."

"Rockpool it is," said Twig. He had to agree that
Vile and the gnome were right. A lost prince? A damsel
in distress? That flyer was the best job option they'd

seen since leaving the Euphonium. Here was a chance to use his powers for something noble and good! And, hopefully, get paid enough to eat.

IN WHICH NO ONE IS EATEN

Rockpool was a mostly unremarkable kingdom. It was larger than Twig's home of Muckwood (as almost all the other kingdoms were), but smaller and less grand than Aramore. But it was on the coast and enjoyed a small amount of success by facilitating trade between the more land-bound kingdoms and the denizens of the Deep Sea. It wasn't unusual to see mermaids, selkies and even some of the elusive blue men wandering the streets. There were even special water-filled carts for rent at the port for visiting mermaids to travel about in comfort.

It was well past midday when they trudged into

town, Beaky now small enough to ride on Twig's shoulder, though he decided to perch atop his head instead.

"Can you get him on my shoulder?" Twig asked Glimfinkle. "People are staring."

"Don't see wot's the problem," said the gnome. He was sitting on Beaky's back. "Besides, I can see where we're goin' from up here. Can't see a thing from yer pocket."

Parchment posters like the one Vile had found in Fallow were plastered everywhere around the city. King Jasper certainly wanted to find his son.

Vile's stomach let out a loud gurgle. "Sooner we get there, sooner we can eat. They'll feed us up front, right?"

Beaky squawked. It had just enough of his boobrie bellow left in it that the people walking in front of them suddenly had somewhere else to be.

"They'd better," said Glimfinkle. "Or else there's gonna be trouble." He patted Beaky. "Turn left up ahead, Twig. Yer almost there."

Coquina Castle came into view as they rounded

the corner. It was a squat stone castle that would have been ugly if not for the colourful shells and sea glass that covered the three large towers. Two guards in full livery were patrolling in front of the wooden drawbridge that crossed the seawater-filled moat. Twig could see the silvery flash of fins swimming back and forth in the water. They were very large and surely attached to something best left alone.

He walked up to the nearest guard. "Hello, we're here about the ... er ... help wanted poster."

The guard eyed the magpie perched on top of his head dubiously. "Cook don't allow pets in the castle kitchen, not unless you want 'em cooked."

Beaky let out an indignant squawk that sounded a good deal like a threat even if you didn't speak magpie. The guard put a hand on the hilt of his sword.

"Hang on now, yer not eatin' Beaky!" Glimfinkle shook a tiny fist right in the guard's face. "I'll have him gobble ye up first! Don't think he won't!"

The other guard strode over to see what was going on. Twig held up his hands. "Slow down a minute," he said. "Nobody's eating anybody." He saw Vile's fingers

34

twitching out of the corner of his eye and elbowed her. "Or cursing anybody or doing *anything* to anybody. We don't want any trouble."

Vile and Glimfinkle both snorted at the same time.

Twig spoke up louder. "We're talking about the reward poster for finding Prince Igneous?" He pulled the crumpled parchment out of his pocket and showed it to the guards.

"You lot?" The guards looked at each other and then they both fell about laughing. Twig grabbed Vile's hand in his to stop her from cursing them then and there. They really needed a paying job, and this was the only lead they had. She was always extra touchy when she was hungry.

"Yes, *us*," said Vile. She drew herself up as tall as possible. "I'm Vile Hornwort, of the Hornwort Hags. Perhaps you've heard of us. I recently won the Euphonium hag scrap."

The guards stopped laughing and one of them took a step back. They'd obviously heard of the Hornworts.

"I see you've heard of me. And," continued Vile grandly, with a sweep of her hand, "*this* is the wizard

Twig Thicket, who just won the Euphonium wizard duel, beating Kudzu of the Spire."

The first guard squinted at Twig. "I heard about that," he said. "Voted Stupidest Wizard, weren't you?"

Twig tried, mostly successfully, to wipe the involuntary grimace off his face. They needed to get inside if they were going to get this job.

"For giving all his magic away," said the other guard.

"Yeah, that was pretty daft," said the first one.

"Hey—" Twig started to say, but the gnome interrupted him.

"He didn't give it all away," snapped Glimfinkle. "He's not *that* dozy. And I, by the way, am the Great Glimfinkle!"

The guards peered at the gnome. "Yeah? And what's so great about you, gnome? You a wee little wizard too?"

Glimfinkle sputtered.

"Anyway," said Twig, trying to get things back on track, "we're here to see the king. We're going to rescue Prince Igneous."

The guards shrugged in unison again. "You and

every other knight errant in the kingdoms," said one. He hitched his head towards the castle entrance. "Go on in. You'll see the queue."

"The queue?" Twig's stomach sank.

"Yeah, the queue. It's what happens when you offer someone's weight in gold as a reward. Half the battalion is off after it." The guards each nodded and returned to their back-and-forth patrol without another word.

"Did he say the reward was yer weight in gold?" Glimfinkle couldn't keep the tinge of awe out of his voice.

"He did," said Vile. She sounded as impressed as the gnome.

"Twig," said Glimfinkle fervently, "quick, magic yerself some really big fat muscles. Or just fat. That'd work too. And can ye make me about quadruple me size?"

* * *

The queue inside the castle was long and mostly made up of a motley assortment of knights in plate armour, but also brawny farmhands and an axe-wielding huntsman or two. Twig only saw one other person who looked like they might be a wizard, but he was also quite fit and carrying a thick staff that looked like it could knock out an ogre in one blow. Twig was definitely the only one accompanied by a hag, a gnome and a magpie.

They joined the end of the queue behind a scrawny knight with rather dented armour.

"Hello there," said the knight, giving them a clanky bow that almost toppled him over. "I am Sir Thinly of Bragmore. And who might you be?"

Twig started to introduce himself, but Vile shouldered him aside and announced, loudly enough for everyone to hear, "This is the great and powerful Wizard Twig, and I am Vile Hornwort of the Hornwort Hags."

"And Glimfinkle the Grand!" chimed in the gnome. Twig tried not to roll his eyes. The two of them were getting less humble every time they introduced themselves.

"A pleasure to meet you all," said the knight, and then jumped as if a nixie had taken a bite out of him.

"Wizard Twig, did you say?"

"Yes. . ." said Twig.

"And Vile the hag?"

Twig nodded with a sinking feeling in his stomach. He thought he knew where this was going. Anyone from the Kingdom of Bragmore probably knew who he was, and Vile too, after what had happened at the Euphonium.

"You're the one that defeated our Wizard Sumac at the Euphonium."

Twig nodded, keeping his chin up. He'd do it again, too. Sumac was a coward and a cheat.

The knight bent down to look at Vile, holding his visor up with one finger. "So I'm guessing that must mean you're the hag that cursed him and turned him into a chicken?"

Vile gave him a very toothy smile and wiggled her fingers in his face. "I am," she said. "What of it?"

"Oh, you'll hear naught from me," said Sir Thinly mildly, though Twig noticed he shifted sideways away from Vile a bit. "Sumac Crabapple was not well-loved in Bragmore."

"Not surprised," said Twig, though he was a little relieved to hear it.

"Though it has put King Egon in a terrible temper, which is why I'm out questing." The knight put a finger to his long, thin nose. "Safer than being at home. The king is interviewing new wizard applicants now and he's not been pleased. There are not many wizards like Sumac Crabapple."

"Thank the heavens fer that," said Glimfinkle.

"Er ... no offence intended," said Twig, "but you don't much seem like you'd ... um ... enjoy working with a wizard like Sumac."

"Yeah," said Vile. "You seem pretty *nice*." Twig couldn't tell if she meant that as a compliment or not.

"One cannot help where one is born, I suppose," said Sir Thinly. "Though, as you can see, my family has fallen on hard times." He motioned towards his dull, dented armour. "I fear I'm not really quite cut-throat enough for King Egon or Bragmore, but recent developments have given me a chance to prove myself."

"Recent developments?" The queue moved and they all shuffled forward.

"Have you not heard?" Sir Thinly's eyebrows rose so far up that they were lost in his helm. "There's a dearth of both knights and princes across the kingdoms at the moment."

"A dearth?" Glimfinkle asked. "Wot's that?"

Twig was glad he'd asked. He wasn't entirely sure what it meant either.

"Meaning," said Sir Thinly, "that a veritable slew of the kingdom's most decorated knights and princes, not to mention a handful of dukes and barons, have all gone missing in the last couple of moons. Crown Prince Igneous is just one of the missing. Why, Bragmore's own Prince Darrold has also disappeared. He vanished without a trace." He paused and looked a little chagrined. "I suppose I should be out looking for *him*, but King Egon has promised no reward, not like King Jasper of Rockpool."

"Where've they all gone?" asked Vile.

"If anyone knew that," said Sir Thinly, "we wouldn't be here. At any rate, it's quite good for questing if you're a lesser knight like myself and these others. We are, I'm afraid, the bottom of the barrel."

Twig took a good look around. Now that he was closer, he could see what Sir Thinly meant. Very few of the knights ahead of them in the queue were decently equipped. Some looked decidedly out of shape. Some were really a bit old to be out questing. And quite a lot of the people waiting weren't knights. Perhaps the flyer hadn't been joking about the reformed highwaymen part. A few didn't look reformed at all. They just looked like bandits.

IN WHICH THERE IS
NOT A PRINCE

At long last, they were ushered into the throne room.
King Jasper sat upon a very sturdy throne made of
rock. He was equally solid, with a squarish head that
seemed to sit directly upon his shoulders. Twig couldn't
help but be reminded of the last time he'd been in a
similar situation, when he'd been called in to meet
the king of Muckwood and ordered to compete in the
Euphonium. At least King Jasper was almost the exact
opposite of King Mervyn, who was all sharp angles
and points, but the expression on his face wasn't much
friendlier. Of course, it wasn't exactly a happy occasion.

"The queen's at least half siren. I'd bet on it," whispered Vile, poking him with her elbow.

Queen Coral sat in a dainty carved stone chair next to the king. Her long dark hair seemed to float about her. Her shining eyes were dark blue-green pools and you could hardly tear your eyes away from them. But she was also the saddest person Twig thought he had ever seen. A fog of regret seemed to surround her. She wore a dark purple and black dress that made her pale, heart-shaped face stand out.

Twig straightened his back and threw back his shoulders, trying to look as impressive as possible. Maybe he should have taken Glimfinkle's advice and added in some muscles.

"Flutter," he whisper-spelled out of the corner of his mouth. His cloak made

of clouds that he'd magicked up especially for the Euphonium obediently flapped and snapped behind him.

"Show-off," muttered Glimfinkle from his pocket.

"The wizard Twig Thicket, Vile Hornwort of the Hornwort Hags, Glimfinkle the Grandiose, and ... Beaky," announced the herald.

"You're calling *me* the show-off?" whispered Twig to Glimfinkle as he bowed low. Beaky, still on his head, flapped a bit and somewhat ruined the effect he was going for.

"A wizard, a hag ... and a gnome?" The king's voice was deep and full of gravel. And doubt.

"You may have heard of us, your kingship," said Vile. "Did you attend this year's Euphonium?" She stood, boots firmly planted, chin up. Twig wondered how she could have so much confidence when he was technically the only one of them that had ever been in a throne room before.

"Your name does proceed you," said Queen Coral. Her lilting voice was like running water and Twig felt a shiver go up his spine. She sounded as sad as she looked.

It made him feel like crying. He cleared his throat.

"We've come to pledge our services. We will find Prince Igneous," he said, a little more loudly than he had intended.

"I see," said King Jasper. "I will tell you as I told the others, he was last seen headed towards the Seven Sisters in the dead of night almost a moon ago. He had been talking for days of a damsel in distress that he needed to save. He took very little with him, just the clothes on his back. We only have this much information because one of the guardsmen attempted to delay him, fearing the worst."

"Could be the sirens at the Seven Sisters..." Vile trailed off, glancing at the queen.

"Not my son," said Queen Coral in a tone that brooked no argument. Vile nodded like she'd known that already.

"Ask 'im about the gold," hissed Glimfinkle in a stage whisper.

"Shh!" said Twig.

But the king had heard. He sighed. "I can only hope you succeed where our own knights have failed. We have also not heard any word from our kingdom's wizard, Chert Boulderwort, who went out searching for the prince immediately. It is not like him at all. He is a venerable and much-trusted wizard with years of experience, though he has never won the Euphonium, like yourself." He rubbed a large hand over the stubble on his chin. "But, if you do manage to find the prince and return him to us, the reward is your weight in gold."

"Our weight ... tha's hardly fair," said Glimfinkle, far too loudly. "Not when we're competin' with full-grown knights in their heavy armour!" He rubbed his little hands together.

"Glimfinkle!" said Twig, and tried to poke the gnome down into his pocket. Even Vile looked slightly shocked.

"What is it you suggest, little one?" asked the queen. Twig felt the tingle down his spine again.

Glimfinkle shoved Twig's hand away. "I'm not asking much, y'see. Just throw in a grand dinner ... and ... Beaky's weight too." He grinned. "In that order, your lordships."

Twig wasn't sure he liked that. They didn't need to be greedy – just fed – and Beaky's weight when he was a boobrie was surely well beyond a knight in full plate armour. It didn't feel fair. He opened his mouth to disagree, but Vile elbowed him.

"That is acceptable," said King Jasper, sounding tired. "Once you have returned our son to us. I would rather have my son back than all the gold in the kingdoms."

"We will be grateful beyond words," added the queen.

Twig swallowed. They *had* to find Prince Igneous. "We will return him to you," said Twig. "*I swear it.*" A small shower of sparks appeared out of nowhere above him and shone in the air for a moment, making Beaky squawk.

They bowed themselves out of the throne room, the king and queen watching them go.

"What was that about?" asked Vile. "You didn't have to set off fireworks."

"I didn't mean to," said Twig. He had a feeling now that this was a promise he *had* to keep. He'd sworn to it with all the magic inside him and he wouldn't be able to rest until it was done.

"Well, no matter," said Glimfinkle. "Now we just need to find ourselves a prince! And make sure Beaky eats his fill before any weighin' goes on!"

* * *

They ran into Sir Thinly as they crossed the castle courtyard, the knight packing up his saddlebags.

"Well met again. Are you off this evening or are you waiting until morning?" asked the knight.

It was nearing sunset and they still hadn't eaten. Twig looked at the others. "I wouldn't mind an actual bed tonight, if we can find an innkeeper to trade with."

"And some supper." Vile scratched her head. Her hair was full of sticks and leaves again, though where she'd picked them up, Twig couldn't even imagine. They'd only walked through tall grass to get to Rockpool.

"And a proper bath," he added. "Who knows when we'll be able to get another one."

"Wouldn't mind a nice warm teacup to soak in

meself," said Glimfinkle. "After that supper, that is."

"Ah, well, I'm off to the Seven Sisters tonight," said Sir Thinly. "I think the rest have already headed that way. Won't do to dawdle with this much competition. Best of luck to you." He bowed to them and clanked off, leading a horse nearly as thin as himself.

"Do you think we ought to head out too?" asked Twig.

"Nah," said Vile. "The prince has been gone ages. One more night won't make much difference. Or one more knight." She laughed at her own joke. "Besides, none of them have what we have."

"Which is?"

"The world's greatest wizard *and* the world's best hag, of course!"

Twig followed as Vile led the way. How could she be so confident? Just this morning they were out of both food and gold, and they weren't much better off now, other than having a job . . . in which all of their competition was technically ahead of them.

"And the best gnome and magpie!" Glimfinkle looked annoyed. "Ye keep fergettin' about us." Beaky let out a gargling bellow of agreement.

"Oh, I couldn't forget you," said Vile, "even if I tried."

"Look, there's an inn!" Twig rushed off ahead before another argument could start up.

The closest inn to the castle was called the Parrot's Tale and it looked a cheery sort of place. Tubs of seawater were placed all around it, and someone had put a magic spell on them so that tiny waves played around the surface of each. The tubs were full of small sea creatures like crabs, snails and tiny little fish swimming merrily to and fro.

Twig brushed himself off, poked Glimfinkle down into his pocket again, and went to find the innkeeper. She was easy to find as she had a brightly coloured parrot perched on her shoulder. The

parrot and Beaky eyed each other up as Twig approached.

"Oooh, I do like a man with a

bird," said the innkeeper. She looked about the same age as his mum, but much more capable. She wore clothes fit for a pirate and her arms bulged with muscles. She held out a hand to Twig. "Name's Bonny. Bonny the Lass."

He shook it, trying not to wince. She had a firm grip. "Twig, Twig Thicket," he said. "And this is Vile," he added as the hag came up behind him. "I'm a wizard. And we were wondering if we could trade some magic—"

"Or curses," said Vile, "if you're wanting anyone covered in boils."

Bonny laughed. "As tempting as that is, the locals know enough not to cross me. Now, what kind of magic are we talking, young wizard? And what are you wanting?"

Twig took a deep breath. So far, so good. At least she hadn't laughed like people often did, saying they were awfully young to be peddling magic. "We could use a place to stay for the night and a supply of food."

"Loads o' victuals!" piped up Glimfinkle. "And mebbe some pudding!"

Twig cleared his throat and firmly put a hand over his pocket, ignoring Glimfinkle's kick. "Perhaps I could trade you some handy things for the kitchen? Some self-stirring spoons for your soup pot? An apron that won't stain? A money pouch that'll spit out false gold coins?" He'd had some success trading those things before in other towns, though he was already tired of making such stuff. He rather hoped she'd ask for something harder and more interesting than he'd ever tried before. *That* was how you learned.

Bonny looked him up and down for a long moment. "An interesting proposition indeed," she said. "Why don't you sit down for some supper while I think on it."

"Done!" Vile plopped herself down at the nearest empty table.

Twig took the seat next to her, plucking out the gnome and setting him down on the table. He took out a couple of sticks and shells and magicked up a small chair and table for the gnome to use. Soon they were all feasting on the best meal any of them had eaten in a very long time. Steaming hot fish and prawn pie, bread with thick slabs of creamy butter, and fresh-pressed apple juice. Bonny even gave a serving of fruit and veg to Beaky without them asking.

When they had finished, Bonny sat down next to them. "So," she said, "been thinking on your offer. I've got myself a storm glass already so I can prepare for the odd squall we get here on the coast." She pointed to a large teardrop-shaped glass container on a shelf next to the door. The water inside it was swirling ever so slightly. "But I've a wonder whether a wizard such as yourself could make something to predict trouble of a more two-legged variety." She gave a pointed look around the room, especially at a few overly happy rough-looking characters in a corner. "I get my fair share of pirates and the like and if you've never seen a merman drunk on elderberry wine, count yourself lucky."

Twig took a last swallow of apple juice to give himself a moment to think. "I've never done anything like that, but I can give it a try." He smiled to himself. A real challenge for once!

"Nothin's impossible fer us," said Glimfinkle. Then he burped. "Take me, I didn't think there were any way

I could finish off that pie, but I did it!"

"We never doubted you," said Vile. "Trust me."

Twig took out a bit of parchment and scribbled down a few possible rhymes. He tried to look wizard-y and thoughtful as he did so until Vile asked him if the fish pie was coming back up on him.

"I think I've got it," he said, standing up. He cleared his throat and waved his hands about a bit, mostly for show.

> *"When trouble is brewing,*
> *And anger is stewing,*
> *Give us a warning,*
> *Be it evening or morning."*

A trickle of sparkles left his fingertips and danced about the air, then settled on to the storm glass and sunk into it, disappearing.

"Is that it?" Glimfinkle belched. "Wot's it do?"

Twig ignored the gnome and turned to Bonny. "It should change colour now, but the storm-predicting part should still be the same. I figured since it's near the door, as people go through, it'll let you know if there's trouble."

"Oooh," she said. "I want to test it!" She strode to the door and took a look outside, then let out a shrill whistle. "Hey, yo! Needle, get over here, I got something to say about your manky, mangy mutt and I wanna say it right to your silly face!" She smiled over her shoulder at them. "Needle's got an anger problem and he does love that dog of his." She stepped back a few steps, waiting with her hands on her hips.

A tall, thin man came storming through the door a moment later. The entire pub watched as the storm glass lit up with a reddish-orange glow.

"Wot'd you say about my Pepper?!"

"Oh, naught," said Bonny the Lass. "Just that I've got a couple bones saved up for the old dear. You want 'em?" She gave the man a cheery smile and waved a hand at one of her servers, who hustled off to the kitchen, presumably in search of some fresh bones.

"Oh, well, then," said Needle, deflating like the wind had gone out of his sails. The storm glass's red glow faded and went a lovely shade of blue, then all the way back to clear. He gave Bonny a confused look and then sat down at a table.

Twig let out the breath he'd been holding. The spell *had* worked. Vile dragged Glimfinkle out from behind the water pitcher where the gnome had taken cover. Bonny clapped Twig on the back. "Looks like it does what it should, lad," she said. "That's some excellent wizarding. Now, come on this way and I'll find you lot a room. And maybe you can do me up a few of those self-stirring spoons in the morning."

As Twig and Vile followed Bonny, they passed near the door. The storm glass suddenly turned a deep, dark, angry-looking red. They looked at each other and Bonny looked at them.

"What's going on here?" she asked, looking at them suspiciously.

"I don't know," said Twig. Had he done something wrong in the spell? Did it just always turn red when someone walked near it? Unless Vile was planning some trouble? But she had a full stomach, so the chances of that were slim.

Then there came a loud, angry squawk from

outside, followed first by a *squelch* and then a smell like all the rotten eggs in the world had exploded at once. And then Twig knew why the storm glass had gone red. Trouble had found them again.

5

IN WHICH THERE IS
SOMETHING ROTTEN

A speckled brown-and-green egg came hurtling through the door, hitting Bonny square in the chest. It exploded and a rotten, sulphurous stench filled the room. The smell was so bad you could almost see it. Twig could taste it. For a moment, he thought the fish pie *would* come back up on him.

"It's that boggin' chicken again!" Glimfinkle voluntarily ducked down all the way into Twig's pocket.

Vile ran through the door, yelling at the top of her lungs, which made a considerable noise. "Sumac, I'm going to curse you so bad that your boils are going to have boils!" Beaky, who had grown a fair amount after his meal, flew after her, bellowing. A flurry of squawks and screeches receded down the street as Vile gave chase.

"What was that?" Bonny looked green. "Was it a . . . chicken? I've never seen a chicken that looked like that. . ." She went to wipe some of the egg off her dress, but then thought better of touching it. The yolk was almost purple and it wobbled, a lot like Sumac's nose boil had once done.

"Um, let me fix that," said Twig.

"Quell this smell!"

A small breeze sprang up and swirled around the room, picking up any gloppy remnants of egg and thankfully whisking away the malodorous odour.

Bonny took a deep breath. "Thanks," she said. "But what brought that . . . that *thing* to my door?"

Glimfinkle popped back up, and before Twig could explain exactly why the ugliest, most foul, boil-covered chicken in all the kingdoms was following them, the gnome said, "That blasted wizard-chicken's got it in fer Twig and Vile both. He's been chucking rotten eggs at us since Vile turned him into a chicken." He poked Twig in the chest. "I'm telling ye, mebbe we *should* let Beaky eat him."

Sumac had cast Nix's Unravelling on Twig during a Euphonium duel and tried to steal his magic from him, nearly killing him in the process. He deserved to be cursed even worse than what he had been, though Twig wasn't sure what that would be. But now it was like Sumac was cursing them back. He had a knack for popping up and egging them at the worst times, like whenever they'd found a nice place to stay for the night.

Twig didn't even protest as Bonny gently but firmly pushed them out the door and slammed it shut behind them. It wasn't the first inn they had been kicked out of since Sumac had started following them around.

He followed the trail of feathers and rotten eggs, cleaning and apologizing as he went. He caught up to Vile and Beaky at the edge of Rockpool near the docks. Vile was shaking her fist at the sky.

"Did ye eat him, Beaky, my boy?" asked Glimfinkle. The magpie-boobrie drooped his head.

"We lost him at the water," said Vile. "Didn't think he'd fly over the Deep Sea, but he did." She brushed her hands together. "But he's a couple of boils heavier and I gave him a mean case of bog itch, so good luck to him scratching without any fingers." She turned to Twig. "I guess we're camping out again tonight, then?"

He nodded. "At least we got a decent meal first," he said.

* * *

The Seven Sisters were actually seven bridges that provided a relatively safe crossing over the Deep Sea to the large rocky island of Bone End. You *could* take a boat from Rockpool to make the journey, but the sea was full of potential terrors and the ship graveyard off the coast was proof of that. The mermaids and blue men had settled into relative peace in recent years, but no one wanted to tangle with the many-eyed morool that patrolled the depths.

The bridges hopped from one large rock outcropping

to another, none of which were much larger than a small hill. The spans had been constructed so long ago, probably by the elves, that no one knew exactly how they had been made or even what they were made of. They gleamed pearly white and sparkled when the sun hit them. Some of them rose so high into the air that the tops were obscured by fog, while a heavy mist usually shrouded the bases.

But the reason they were called the Seven Sisters wasn't because there were seven of them. For as long as anyone could remember, seven sirens had made their homes under the bridges. That's why it was only a *relatively* safe way to get to Bone End. You had to take precautions.

Of course, there wasn't much reason to travel to the island. Bone End was full of rocks and little else. Nothing much grew there except an abundance of rosemary and rock cress, though witches swore by the quality of both. It was a good place to go if you wanted to get away from people. Twig couldn't think of any reason why Prince Igneous would have wanted to go there. Other than the town of Kneecap and some ruins dotted about, he had never heard of anything else noteworthy on Bone End.

After breaking camp, they set off for the Seven Sisters. Beaky was hungry again and only about the size of a sea eagle, so Twig and Vile walked while only Glimfinkle rode on the magpie. Twig was rather glad. Flying wasn't very fun when you were always worried about crashing, and he *really* didn't want to crash into the Deep Sea.

"Do you think you can make it so Beaky's not so hungry all the time?" asked Vile.

"I've been thinking about it," said Twig, "but I'm not sure. I don't want to mess it up." It seemed like some unforeseen side effect always happened when he tried to transform living creatures, even when he tried to reason it out first. It was much safer to cast spells on *things*. Things didn't have opinions and they never argued. Or tried to eat you, except that time he'd accidentally given a chest of drawers some teeth.

Vile was quiet for a few minutes. They had left Rockpool behind and were walking along the coastal path to the beginning of the seven bridges. It reminded

Twig of their first journey together, going through the Withering Swamp to get to Witch Wormwood's house. It felt like that had been for ever ago. He wondered if the shellycoat they had met along the way had made it back home or not. He stopped and picked up a pretty abalone shell from the path. Vile scooped one up too, but she chucked hers into the water with a splash.

"Hey! Watch where you're throwing things!" An angry mermaid popped up out of the sea, Vile's shell perched on top of her green hair. She plucked it off and shook her fist at them.

"Sorry," said Vile. "Didn't see you there."

"Didn't look, more like," said the mermaid. She pulled back her arm like she was going to heave the shell back at them, but then her eyes narrowed. She glared at Twig.

Why was she looking at him? He hadn't been the one to throw the shell. He tried not to stare back. He'd never seen a mermaid before, but he'd heard they could be quite touchy. He'd hoped to catch a faraway glimpse of one in Rockpool, but he hadn't seen any in their short time in the city. This one was entirely too close.

They were known to be beautiful but unpredictable.

The mermaid pulled herself out of the water and on to a flat rock. Her tail was an iridescent green with flecks of silver and turquoise. She wore a sort-of tunic made of knitted seaweed and decorated with pearls and shells.

"Where'd you get that shell?" she asked.

Twig held up the shell he'd picked up. "Just from the path," he said. "I can put it back. I didn't mean any harm ... or ... did you want it?" He wasn't sure what the proper protocol was to not annoy a mermaid. He looked to Vile, but she just shrugged.

"Not that one," said the mermaid. She tapped near her throat. "The one on your cloak." She was still staring awfully hard at him.

"I didn't steal it!" Twig rubbed the shell. "A shellycoat gave it to me." It was only a common cockle shell, but there had been something about the shape of it that he liked, so he'd used it to make a clasp for his cloak. "He gave me a whole bag. Do you ... do you want one?" He'd used a few of them up for spells, but he still had quite a lot left. They were handy to turn into dinner plates and once he'd used them to make a solid umbrella when it had hailed.

"A shellycoat *gave* them to you?"

"Yeah," said Vile. "Twig here likes to help people out." She didn't make it sound like a good thing.

Twig pulled the bag of shells out. "Would you like one?" At least the mermaid wasn't glaring any more, though she did seem surprised. He took out a long twisty one that had once belonged to a snail. "I could make it into something for you."

> *"I mean you well*
> *with this shell.*
> *Perhaps with this cup*
> *you can sup."*

With a few sparkles, the shell transformed into a dainty goblet. He stepped forward to hold it out to the mermaid.

Vile snorted. "Fat lot of good that'll do someone who lives in the water, Twig."

"Oh," said Twig. He hadn't thought of that. He

looked sadly at the cup. It had turned out quite pretty, with a spiral going all the way up. "Sorry, let me try something else. . ."

But before he could think of another spell or transform the shell back, the mermaid reached out and grabbed it.

"You truly *are* a friend of the waterfolk," she said, holding up the goblet and admiring it in the sun. "You may call me Cassidae."

"Pardon?"

Cassidae smiled at him, all dimples now. It was a smile so brilliant you could almost ignore the fact that

her teeth looked very sharp. "I thought you might have stolen that shell, but it seems it was given to you in good faith."

Vile looked from Twig to the mermaid

and back again. "It's just a shell," she said. "And not even a very pretty one."

"Vile!" Must she always insult everything? Especially now that the mermaid seemed to be friendly. His brother Badger was always going on about mermaids and how beautiful they were, but Twig read books, unlike the rest of his family. He knew what could happen if you got on a mermaid's bad side and it usually involved drowning or their very pointy teeth.

"It is not just a shell," said Cassidae, still admiring the goblet. "Well, that is, it *is* a shell. But it has also been marked to show the bearer is a friend. It will give you safe passage through most waters."

"Wow," said Twig.

"Really?" said Vile. "Now, that's worth something."

The mermaid turned her glare to the hag. Her clear blue eyes suddenly glinted red, but it was gone so quickly that Twig thought it might have been a trick of the light. "It must not be sold," she said.

"Oh, I wouldn't!" Twig elbowed Vile. "We wouldn't, would we, Vile?"

"No, of course not," said Vile, elbowing him back.

"Too useful. We're likely going to need it crossing the Seven Sisters."

Cassidae shook her head. "*You* may be marked as a friend," she said, looking just at Twig, "but that doesn't mean all waterfolk are friendly. Be wary going over the Seven Sisters. Sirens are as changeable as the sea. And they're not truly waterfolk, anyway." She sniffed. "Feathery creatures, always snatching all the good travellers with their silly songs."

"Thanks for the warning," said Twig, backing away just a little.

"Though you are in luck today," continued the mermaid. "It's market day in the Cove and the girls are likely to be out shopping. They do like a bargain."

"Perfect," said Twig. Mermaids were one thing, but sirens were another thing entirely. Part woman, part bird, from what he'd heard. It was hard to imagine what they looked like, even after seeing the queen, but she'd been only part siren and covered up to boot. He'd already made himself up some earplugs out of a twist of cloth, but now he wouldn't have to wear them.

Cassidae disappeared into the water with a flick of

her tail, managing to splash Vile right in the face.

"Blegh!" Vile spat out some seawater. "Stupid fish!"

A shell broke the water and sailed through the air to peg the hag right in the middle of her forehead. Twig just managed not to laugh.

6

IN WHICH THINGS
GO TOO FAST

They caught up with Glimfinkle and Beaky at the base
of the first of the bridges. Beaky was eating something
with greenish-purple tentacles as they walked up.

"Wot took ye so long?" asked Glimfinkle. He was
sitting well off to the other side of the rock from the
now quite large magpie. Coarse black boobrie feathers
had begun sprouting.

"Met a mermaid," said Vile. "And *we* weren't flying."

"Well, *we* met a sea creature o' some sort,
but ye can see how that went." Glimfinkle gave
an involuntary shiver and nodded towards the

fast-disappearing tentacle.

Beaky finished slurping it up like a worm and then gave a very non-magpie sounding burp. Vile glanced pointedly at Twig. Twig looked away.

"So," he said brightly, "who's ready for the Seven Sisters?"

As if on cue, a shaft of sunlight broke through the mist and fog, making the first bridge gleam in front of them. It was one of the shorter spans, if Twig remembered correctly, and the one you were least likely to run into trouble on. He touched the shellycoat's shell at his throat and put on a big smile for his travelling companions.

"Eh, I'm flyin'," said Glimfinkle. "Looks a long slog, that. We'll see ye on the other side." The gnome clambered up the rock and on to Beaky's back. He tipped his hat to them as Beaky flew off, leaving behind a few long black feathers.

"Didn't even ask if we wanted a ride, that selfish little gnome," said Vile. "Beaky was almost big enough."

"Yeah, but..." Twig mimed them falling and released a little spell to make a *SPLASH* noise followed by some *GURGLE, GURGLE, GLUB, GLUB* sounds.

"Point taken," said Vile. "Let's walk."

They started up the first bridge. The path was very clear, with no stray rocks or pebbles or even cracks in the glittering white stone. And no one else was walking it. Their footsteps seemed to echo.

It was a steep enough climb that they saved their breath until stopping at the top to take a break. Vile leaned against the low stone wall that ran along the edge of the bridge and wiped the sweat off her forehead. Twig flopped down beside her.

"Why, exactly, are we doing this?" Vile sounded annoyed, which was pretty much her normal tone of voice.

"To get to the other side? To save a prince and return him to his family? To have an adventure?" Twig was sure that if Glimfinkle had been there, he'd have added, "To get our weight in gold!"

"No, I mean, you're the world's greatest wizard. We're only halfway over the first bridge and I'm wheezing like a banshee with a cold. WHY ARE WE WALKING?"

"Oh, right," said Twig. He almost added that it hadn't even occurred to him to magic them across, but he didn't feel like having Vile hex him. He stood up and looked about for inspiration. It might be one of the shorter spans, but it still looked a long way down.

"Let's glide
Down this slide."

He took Vile's hand in his own, took a deep breath, and stepped forward. At first nothing seemed to happen, and then suddenly they were travelling along without moving their feet. Slowly at first and then faster and faster until the air was whipping them in the face. They reached the rocks at the bottom of the first bridge, but instead of slowing down, they sped up as they started up the next.

Twig got a mouthful of Vile's hair and spat it out. He narrowed his eyes against the wind. They were going so fast that they were leaving a Vile and Twig shaped hole in the mist and clouds as they sped through. Tears were starting to form in his eyes. He wasn't even sure which of the bridges they were on now. He clung on to Vile's hand, afraid they would be torn apart. He wasn't sure what would happen if they got separated, but he was pretty sure it wouldn't be good. He had a sudden image of them flying off the bridge in opposite directions.

"Make. It. Stop!" Vile shouted.

"That's enough of this ride!"

The spell abruptly ended as the words left Twig's mouth and they tumbled to the ground in a heap. Vile sat up and whacked him on the shoulder. "The next time I ask you to use your magic, just say no."

"Sorry," said Twig, for probably the gazillionth time. Maybe he should have tried going back to Muckwood to learn to control his power better, not that Ripplemintz the Sage had ever taught him much of anything when he had worked as his apprentice. Ripplemintz wasn't a very good wizard. That was how he'd wound up in Muckwood. But King Mervyn had been clear Twig wouldn't be coming back as an apprentice anyway – he wanted the Euphonium winner for court wizard of his kingdom.

It was all well and good that Witch Wormwood had told him that doing was the best way of learning, but she wasn't the one nearly getting splatted or eaten or drowned when one of his spells went wonky.

Vile clambered to her feet and held out a hand to Twig. "Come on, don't mope. I didn't mean it. It's not your fault you're the greatest-most-rubbish wizard in all the kingdoms."

He took her hand and let her haul him to his feet.

"Whose fault is it if it isn't mine?"

"No one's," said Vile, clapping him on the back. "You just need more practice on the small stuff so the big stuff doesn't get so . . . big. Or the small stuff doesn't wind up big. Whatever. Where are we, anyway?"

Twig walked to the edge and looked back. "Wow," he said, "we're almost at the end of the sixth bridge. There's just one more span to go."

"And we didn't die or go hurtling off into the Deep Sea! Yay, Twig!" She clapped.

Sometimes, he really couldn't tell when she was

joking and when she wasn't.

"Let's just get going," he said, and trudged off. His head was still spinning from the spell, but he'd rather not rest until they were on solid ground. He hadn't told Vile, but he didn't actually know how to properly swim. The biggest bodies of water he'd grown up around had been a kelpie-infested pond and the castle moat, which was home to Fred, an overfed aquatic dragon. Neither one was safe to swim in. In fact, drowning was likely your best option since it was a step up from being swallowed alive.

"Hey," said Vile, "isn't that Sir Thinly? Or rather, his horse?"

Twig looked at where she was pointing. The small round island that marked the end of the sixth bridge and the beginning of the seventh was full of rocks in various sizes. A thin old grey mare with its saddle still on was chewing fitfully on the only tuft of grass left. A familiar looking beat-up shield with the Bragmore crest lay near the edge of the water.

"Sir Thinly? Are you there, Sir Thinly?" Twig called, softly at first, in case the knight was just resting, and then louder. He walked cautiously towards the shield. It was awfully near the water. From what he could see of it through the mist, the water was a dark impenetrable blue. Didn't that mean it was deep there?

Vile went up to the horse and patted it on its velvety nose. She took a sugar cube out of their Pixie Post stash and gave it to the mare. "Did that silly old knight just leave you here?"

"I doubt he'd do that," said Twig. If the spell hadn't zoomed them here, they'd still be on the second bridge. There was no way anyone would abandon a horse to walk on foot across the Seven Sisters. Especially if they were wearing armour.

"Probably a siren got him," said Vile. "Doubt if he has some friend of the waterfolk badge to rely on." She checked the horse over. "She's in good shape for an old girl. I bet she could carry us both."

"Vile!"

"What? You'd rather just leave her here for whatever got Sir Thinly?"

"No! But . . . no!" He shook his head. How could Vile be so . . . practical? He stomped over to the shield, looking around for any other sign of the knight. "Hello! Is anyone there?!"

He saw a gauntlet lying half in the water, but the mist was growing thicker by the minute and he couldn't see much beyond the outstretched fingertips. Twig gulped and crept closer. Now he wasn't sure if he was hoping Sir Thinly was still wearing the gauntlet or not. "Sir Thinly?"

The gauntlet twitched and Twig nearly jumped out of his skin. He leapt forward and grabbed it without thinking. "Sir Thinly!"

Now he could see the knight's head, which was barely sticking out of the water as the waves lapped against him. The mist gathered thickly about him like a damp blanket, almost like it was holding him down. Twig pulled with all of his might, but all that happened was the gauntlet came off. He threw it over his shoulder and grabbed on to the knight's cold hand. "Vile, come help!"

"Yes, do," came a raspy, sickly sweet sing-song voice that seemed to come from everywhere and nowhere. "Come closer, do, I want to get to know *yoooouuuu. . .*"

A pale hand sprang out of the mist and grabbed Twig's wrist in a tight grip. He tried to pull back, but it was no use. The hand felt like ice, with fingernails like talons and small feathers that pricked him. "Yes, you, you pretty, pretty *foooooooool...*" A face appeared, almost like the mist had rolled back to reveal it. A pale, beautiful-but-grim face with a thin, pointed nose and eyes as deep, dark and still as the sea. The siren smiled at Twig, her lips blood red, revealing teeth like pearls. "Come and join me, *doooooooo...*"

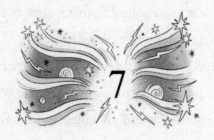

IN WHICH THERE IS A
FALSE NOTE

Twig felt a shiver up and down his spine, a bit like the one he'd felt when talking with Queen Coral. But where it had felt a bit thrilling before, now he was filled with something else. He couldn't even put a name on it. It was like wanting something and needing it, but being terrified of whatever it was at the same time. A lump like lead settled into his stomach. He felt like he would sink straight to the bottom of the Deep Sea if he even took one step towards the water.

"Come with me and you'll *seeeeee*," sang the siren.

"Twig! Shut your ears! Don't you listen to her!" Vile's

voice felt like it was coming from a long way away.

"You need to know how to *controooooollll. . .*"

Control! Yes, that was exactly what he needed. He had to learn how to control his magic or he was going to wind up getting them all killed some day. He let go of Sir Thinly's hand, not even sure why he'd been holding it in the first place. What was Sir Thinly doing here anyway?

"If you only knew, what you could *dooooooo. . .*"

Twig felt something shaking him. Was that Vile? But all he could see was the siren's face. Why had he thought it scary? Now that he was closer, he could see that she was kind and full of knowledge. She would be able to help him. She could teach him what he needed to know so he'd stop making mistakes.

"Just come with me, into the *seaaaa. . .*"

As the last note left her lips, her face twisted in pain. She took her hand off of Twig and clutched at her throat. "Come. . ." she tried to sing, but instead fell into a fit of violent coughing. *"Coff chak coff grakkk coff!"*

Twig blinked. And then he flinched as Vile stuffed something that went *goosh* and *squelch* in his ears so hard that it made his head ring.

"Ow!" His voice was muffled even to himself. "What was that for?"

Vile stuck her face right in his. "For being stupid!" She was obviously shouting, but he could barely hear her.

Twig was about to argue when he realized he was half in the water. He scrambled backwards, scuttling over the rocks, until he was a safer distance away. He could barely hear it now, but the siren was still coughing. She was doubled over, her face red. She reminded him of the castle cat when it hacked up a hairball.

The siren didn't seem very tall or dangerous as she flailed around. Her hair, like Queen Coral's, floated eerily about her. Feathers covered her arms and torso, though she was mostly human shaped, except for her legs and feet, which were birdlike. A very large bird, not unlike Beaky when he was part of the way to being a boobrie. Her face was human enough, though her nose had a hawk-like quality to it. The sharpened talons on her fingertips, however, weren't very human at all.

85

Twig pulled his wrist to his chest. It throbbed in pain. He shook his head. He could still hear the melody of the song she'd been singing, though now he couldn't remember the words. What had she said? Why had he been so willing to follow her?

Whatever Vile had jammed in his ears was starting to ooze back out. He could hear the *"Coff ehHKkkk coff coff"* of the siren more clearly now. He needed to clear his head. He felt out of focus and bleary.

Vile had pulled Sir Thinly completely out of the water and taken his helm off all by herself. Twig couldn't hear what she was saying, but he could tell by the way her lips moved that she was muttering to herself the entire time. He was almost glad he couldn't hear her because he was pretty sure it wasn't anything kind. She was trying to get the knight's pauldrons off now, without much success.

He stood up and walked over, wanting to help. "What can I do?" he yelled.

Vile grimaced at him. "Do something useful," she yelled back and pointed at the siren.

Twig gulped. What kind of useful thing did she

mean? The siren was still clutching her throat, her face nearly purple. He tiptoed nearer.

"I ... *coff* ... can't ... *coff* ... stop..." From what he could hear through the goop, her voice was a deep-throated rasp. It gave him shivers.

He dug into his pocket and pulled out one of Witch Wormwood's dragon mints. He took a deep breath. "Do you promise not to sing if I help you?"

The siren nodded, her eyes watering. Twig held out the dragon mint and she snatched it from him and shoved it into her mouth. Her coughing slowed down and then stopped just a few moments later. She sucked on it in silence, staring at him like she was measuring him up.

Twig backed a few steps away, wiping at some of the goo dripping down the side of his face. His hand came away goopy and vaguely greyish-green. He sniffed his fingertips and recoiled in disgust. Slug poultice. Vile had stuffed slug poultice in his ears. She swore by the nasty stuff to cure all manner of ills, but certainly no one had ever had it shoved in their ears before. He almost but not quite wanted to duck his entire head into the Deep Sea, but he didn't trust the siren enough for that. He wasn't going anywhere near the water, not while she was nearby.

"What did you do?" Vile poked him in the shoulder. "How exactly is stopping her cough useful? That cough was the only thing that saved you from drowning yourself." Vile stomped over to the siren. "And, you! What's your problem? What did Sir Thinly and Twig ever do to you?"

"Nothing," the siren said, her voice harsh. Her tongue was bright green now from the dragon mint. She sucked on the mint, making a *thuck, thuck* sound.

"Hang on," said Twig, "Vile, you didn't get mesmerized or whatever too?"

Vile snorted and tossed her hair. "Of course not. One, I'm a hag. Two, I'm a girl. Three, I'm not silly enough to believe in whatever some bird-woman goes singing at me, *especially* if it involves walking into the Deep Sea. I'm practical. Unlike *some* people I could mention."

Twig thought it might be best to change the subject. "Is Sir Thinly OK?" Vile had managed to sit the knight up against a rock, but his eyes were still closed.

It wasn't Vile that answered. "He'll be OK, once he comes round," said the siren. "He had a strong will for a man. And my voice is not its best. I've been trying to get him all night. But I've had a cold." She cleared her throat and took another strong *thuck* on the mint. "Have you got any more of these?"

"But. . ." Twig trailed off. Why *had* he given her one? Wouldn't she just lure more travellers to their doom if he helped cure her cough? Witch Wormwood's dragon mints were really good. Much better than slug poultice or rootwood bark tea.

"My name is Quinsy," said the siren.

"Why do you do it?" Twig asked. Why would anyone choose to lure people to their doom, singing songs of lies and false hope?

Quinsy shrugged, her feathers rippling. "It's in my nature," she said. "What would you have me do, not sing?"

"Yes!" Twig wasn't even sorry that he'd shouted.

"It's up to them to listen or not," she said calmly, her voice less raspy by the minute. "But I must sing for them. Why, just last month there was a lordling come through who had no mind for my song at all."

"But why?" he asked desperately. "*Why* do you have to sing to them?" She must have some kind of reason. She didn't even know him or Sir Thinly. Why lure them to certain death? How many had gone before him?

"Why do you breathe?"

"I have to breathe or I'll die," said Twig, throwing his hands in the air. "But I'm not hurting anyone by *breathing*."

"And *I* must sing to them of their heart's desires," said Quinsy. "It's what I do." She smoothed down the feathers on her torso. "Besides, men are all the same. They just want to plunder and destroy things and kidnap you to do their laundry."

"I can't believe I'm saying this, but how can you say that?" asked Vile. "Did you talk to Twig or Sir Thinly before you started luring them to their doom?"

Quinsy looked a little uncomfortable for the first time. "Well, no . . . but. . ."

Twig couldn't stand still. "I've never wanted to plunder or destroy anything!" He threw his hands in the air. The siren's calmness was making him really angry. How could she just assume that all men were mean and evil? That was like saying all wizards were as bad as Sumac. Sure, OK, maybe half the wizards he'd met so far were jerks, but not all of them.

"And laundry is obviously not on our list of priorities," continued Vile, poking a finger through a hole in her dress.

"But you want control." The siren pointed at Twig.

"Of my magic! So I don't destroy anything by accident!" Vile patted him on the shoulder. He took a deep breath. "And what about Sir Thinly? What did you sing to him about? I bet he didn't want to steal anything either!"

Quinsy shifted back and forth on her bird feet and looked away. She mumbled something.

"What?" said Vile. "I don't think I heard that."

"It was a song ... of hearth and home ... and ... fuzzy kittens."

"Oh, yes," said Vile, "so *totally* evil. I completely see why you felt you needed to drown him immediately."

Quinsy's feathers drooped. "I can't not sing," she said.

"Agreed. You have a lovely voice." Sir Thinly's reedy voice surprised them all. He sounded tired, but surprisingly strong, considering he'd been mostly waterlogged for the better part of a night.

"I do?"

"The most beautiful voice I've ever heard," said Sir Thinly, struggling to stand. Twig hurried over and gave him a shoulder to lean on. "Your song made me wonder what I'm even doing out here questing after some lost prince that I don't really care about when I could be sat at home in front of the fire, enjoying a nice cup of tea." He nodded to Twig and Vile. "I was born to it, but I've never much liked being a knight."

Twig looked at the siren. She was staring at Sir Thinly like she'd never seen a man before. "If you *have* to sing," said Twig, "do you . . . have to sing people, you know, into the sea?"

The siren opened her mouth and then closed it again and then let out a cough. Twig handed her another dragon mint, even though he didn't think she really needed one. Vile rolled her eyes.

"I. . ." Quinsy cleared her throat. "That is. . ."

"I think we can safely say the answer to that is a no," said Vile.

"It's what my mother taught me!" The siren looked back and forth between them, her eyes lingering longest on Sir Thinly. "I thought this is how I'm . . . how I'm *supposed* to be!"

Sir Thinly straightened up, letting go of Twig. "I'm *supposed* to be a knight," he said. "But, you know what? I've always wanted to be a fisherman." He looked out towards the horizon, the sun glinting across the water, and smiled. "I love the sea." He took a shaky step towards Quinsy. "Can you sing that song for me again? That's what I want. A little cottage, a warm fire, a kitten purring on my lap. . ."

"But without the drowning part," said Twig sternly.

8

IN WHICH THERE ARE
NO LEGS IN THE STEW

They left Sir Thinly and Quinsy sitting on a rock next to each other, chatting about small fuzzy animals. Twig dried himself off with a spell and managed to get the last bit of slug poultice out of his ears, though he imagined he could still feel the sliminess deep inside his head. He and Vile began the climb up the last of the Seven Sisters.

"Do you think he'll be OK?" Twig asked. He couldn't help but worry. He'd felt the pull of Quinsy's song and it was strong. If she went back to her old ways. . .

"Eh, maybe. Can an ogre change his warts?"

"That's a little different," said Twig. He hoped.

"True enough. But look at Queen Coral. She seemed happy enough with King Jasper. So it's possible. Maybe."

"You think we should go back for him?"

Vile shook her head. "Nah. He's a grown knight, even if he is only about half as big as a regular one. Besides, didn't you hear what Quinsy said? About some fancy guy that had come through that wouldn't listen to her song? I bet that was Prince Igneous. Since his mum is at least part siren, he wouldn't be affected by their song. She gave us our first real lead!"

"We already knew he came this way," said Twig.

"Yeah, but now we know he made it over the bridges." Vile had a bounce in her step. "I've got a good feeling about this!"

That made Twig very worried somehow.

"Heya!" came a yell from above. Beaky came swooping down to land in front of them, Glimfinkle waving at them. The magpie was nearly as tall as Twig now. "I've been waitin' for ages," said the gnome. "I've already been to Kneecap and back and got us a room at the Shin and Bone."

"We ran into a siren," said Twig.

Glimfinkle squinted at him. "Ye keep havin' all the fun," he said. "Mebbe I shouldn't have flown on ahead."

"Wait, someone rented *you* a room?" Vile giggled. She pinched her fingers together like she was picking up something tiny.

The gnome turned a bit red and glared at her. "None o' yer short jokes," he said. "Besides, the innkeeper's blind as a bat. He thinks I'm a proper big lord, he does. Says there's been an influx of us lately."

"A lord?! You!" Vile nearly fell over laughing.

"Yeah! Promised us a right fancy supper too!" Glimfinkle drew himself up. "As benefitin' a man o' my stature!"

Even Twig had to roll his eyes at that one. They had to wait a good five minutes for Vile to be able to walk again.

* * *

Kneecap was even smaller than Fallow had been. There was only the one inn, the Shin and Bone, and it doubled as a general store that sold only the essentials. The buildings were a hodgepodge, constructed out of whale bones bleached white by the sun and bits of shipwrecks. There was a blacksmith, but the forge wasn't fired. The few scattered houses all faced away from each other, so one door couldn't be seen from another. No one even poked a head out as they walked into town, though Twig saw some curtains twitch.

The Shin and Bone was a mostly wrecked pirate ship, with a crow's nest on top still flying a tattered black skull-and-crossbones flag. The door had once been the jawbone of some very large sea creature, while the windows were old portholes.

"Remember," whispered Glimfinkle as they approached the toothy door, "I'm *Lord* Clickkettle." He was settled in Twig's pocket again, as Beaky had flown off to search for another unfortunate octopus.

The inside of the Shin and Bone was nearly as dark as

a whale's belly, and it stunk of tallow and pitch and fishy things.

"Um, hello?" Twig called into the darkness. He already felt a twinge of guilt. He'd never been good at lying. His brother Badger had tried to teach him, saying it was an essential life skill, but Twig didn't have the stomach for it. In fact, his stomach felt like it was full of nixies.

"Yo, ho!" came a hearty voice. A wiry man with a black bandana tied around his eyes stumped around the corner. His nose was the largest part of him. And one of his legs was made of a piece of carved driftwood. It looked like a sea serpent. "Welcome, welcome, my esteemed guests!" He strode forward with a friendly, gap-toothed smile, hand outstretched.

The innkeeper was not only completely blind, but he only had one leg.

Twig gulped. He looked at Vile. She shrugged.

"Hi, ho!" answered Glimfinkle. "I'm back and I've brought me friends . . . er, me servants wit' me!"

"Glimfinkle!" He couldn't go through with the gnome's plan. Twig hurriedly stepped up to take the man's hand. He shook it. "I'm sorry, um, mister. . .?"

"Oh, I'm no mister! That's fancy talk for the mainland. You're on Bone End now! Just call me Pegfoot!"

"Right, um, Mr Pegfoot. I'm really sorry, but Glimfinkle—"

"Lord Clickkettle to you!" interrupted the gnome.

Twig poked the gnome back down into his pocket. "*Glimfinkle's* not actually a lord. We're just regular travellers. So you don't have to, you know, go to any fuss."

"*Ir*regular travellers, more like," said Vile.

"There goes me good supper," said Glimfinkle glumly from the depths of Twig's pocket.

Pegfoot threw his head back and laughed with all his might. He sounded a bit like a donkey. And he kept laughing until tears leaked out from under his bandana and his guffaw subsided into snorts. "Oh, ho," he finally choked out. "I'm blind, but I wasn't born yesterday! Whoever heard of a little lordling gnome?" That set him off again. They all looked at each other until this round had settled into hiccups.

"How'd ye know I was a gnome?"

"I can smell ya! If it smells like a gnome, lies like a gnome, why, I guess it's a gnome!"

Vile choked back a snort. "I like him," she said. "Pegfoot, did you say?" She gave the man an appraising look. "Not *the* Pegfoot, are you?"

"At your service," he said, and bowed low, just missing the corner of a table with his head.

"Who's Pegfoot?" Twig tried to whisper to her, but the innkeeper heard him anyway.

"Why, that's me! Scourge of the Deep Sea! The Shin and Bone was my ship, back in the day, before I was struck blind in a battle the likes of which has never been seen before – or since!" He waved a scarred hand in the air. "It were me and me crew against a whole shoal of sea worms out for blood!"

"I heard it was the devil whale," said Vile.

"Aye, he was there too!" Pegfoot smiled. "He's the one that got me leg." He hit his hand upon his knee with a dull thunk.

Twig had the feeling that the man would be winking at them if he didn't have the bandana on.

"So, y'see," said Pegfoot, "I'm a man what knows a liar when he smells one."

"Sorry about that," said Twig.

"What're you apologizing for? Weren't your lie, now was it?" Pegfoot leaned forward and took a good sniff. "Now you, you smell as honest as the day is long. Bit wizard-y, though." He took a step back. "Suppose you're here after all the little princelings and whatnot that have come through of late? We haven't had this much traffic in Kneecap since the star fell and brought everyone over lookin' for stardust."

"We're looking for Prince Igneous of Rockpool," said Twig. "He might have come through sometime in the last moon?"

"Biggish bloke with footsteps solid enough to make the tables rock? Smelled a bit like sand?"

"If he's at all like his dad," said Vile.

"Could be, then. He was the same as the rest, mooning about like a lovesick cow. Headed up to the tower like the rest of 'em. Never came back, just like the rest of 'em too."

"The tower?"

101

Pegfoot let out a sigh. "Just like I told the knights that stopped by yesterday. That's where they all go. And that's where they all stay. The Kraken's Toothpick, up the top of Knucklebone Cliff. And that, my irregular friends, is a place best avoided."

"Sounds like it," said Glimfinkle, who'd popped his head back out of Twig's pocket. "Which means it's where we'll be goin', I expect."

"No one's gone to see what happened to everyone?" asked Twig.

"None of my concern," said Pegfoot. "People don't come to Bone End 'cause they want their business known. Besides, we've had enough trouble dealing with the plague of frogs."

"The plague . . . of frogs?"

"Yeah, frogs, toads, whatever. More warts than you can shake a stick at. Dozens and dozens of 'em. Chuck 'em in the pond, and they just hop back out, always tryin' to waltz right in the door like they own the place. Never seen anything like it, and I was here when the puddlefoots tried to take over."

"Hmmm," went Vile. "You got any of these

frogs around?" .

"Not at the moment, but there'll probably be more show up soon," said Pegfoot. "It's been goin' on for a couple of moons now. Me and a few of me old mates managed to round up all the ones we could find. We threw 'em in the Moaning Caves and put up a fence." He tapped a finger against his head. "Now we're probably going to have to rename 'em the Croaking Caves." He laughed at his own joke.

Glimfinkle cleared his throat. "So, about that supper we spoke about earlier—"

"It's not frogs' legs stew, is it?" Vile interrupted.

"Nah, fish stew," said Pegfoot. "But now that you mention it, why didn't I think o' that before?" He made to clap Vile on the back and she ducked just in time to avoid him whacking her in the head. "Clever girl!"

"Hag," she said. "Clever hag."

"Even better," he said. "Never met a hag who couldn't beat me at cards. Now, then, how long you lot wanting the room for?"

9

IN WHICH NO ONE WANTS EGGS FOR BREAKFAST

After supper and a round of unsolicited advice about where not to stick their noses while on Bone End, and elaborate stories about his days of plundering, Pegfoot gave them a room right under the crow's nest to sleep in. Instead of beds, there were hammocks, and the only way to get to the room was by climbing some rigging and going up through a trapdoor. A slight sea breeze blew in through the cracks, gently rocking the hammocks, almost like they were at sea.

Twig had just settled down into his hammock when he felt a familiar tingle in the air.

"Pixie *Pooooosssssttttt!*" Zinnia *POPPED* in right in front of his nose, nearly making him go cross-eyed. He pushed her away, trying to avoid her wings.

"Too close!"

"*De-livery* for Twig Thicket, boy wizard, formerly of Muckwood!"

"Zinnia, seriously," said Vile, already buried deep in her hammock, "we *know*. It's always for Twig. Just give him his message already and get out of here."

The pixie stuck out her lower lip. "I have my *stan-dards*," she trilled.

"Oh, let her talk," said Glimfinkle, who was washing his face in a teacup. "It'll go faster if ye don't argue."

Zinnia shot the gnome a look. Twig wasn't sure if it was a grateful one or not.

"Message from Witch Wormwood of the Withering Swamp!"

It was just as well Witch Wormwood wasn't there in person. She was always full of advice and, while much of it was good, she also wasn't afraid to say exactly what she thought about everything. Twig wasn't sure what she'd think of them having already run out of gold and being kicked out of nearly every inn they'd tried to stay at.

Zinnia took a deep breath, put one hand on her hip and shook a finger at Twig, just like Witch Wormwood would have.

"Dear Twig,
Don't bother
your head about the
Wizard Quarterly
cover. You know what
I think of wizards and
their opinions. Present
company excepted, of course. I
have enclosed some of my prize-winning
dragon mint in case you have run out.
Sincerely yours, Witch Wormwood"

Zinnia bowed in mid-air and then leaned forward. She put a finger against her nose and looked sharply at Twig.

"P.S. Have you figured out yet what the oracle's

last prophecy means? I am most curious. Respond
when you can.

P.P.S. Also, have a word with that blasted wizard
Kudzu. I'm still cutting down gorse bushes and
blackberries after he sent me one of his beauty bombs.
I blame this entirely on you."

Somehow, the little pixie managed to sound just like the witch. She shook herself and then pulled a plain leather pouch out of the air and dropped it in Twig's lap.

"There's your dragon mint! It was quite heavy, you know," said the pixie pointedly. Twig sighed, then dug a sugar cube out of his pocket and handed it over. Zinnia took it with a beaming smile and stuffed the entire thing in her mouth in one go.

It was Glimfinkle's turn to snort. "Wot was that nonsense that silly oracle said again?"

"We must find beauty where there is none," said Twig. He'd been thinking about the oracle's parting prophecy after the Euphonium and couldn't make any sense of it, much like the first ones she had given them. They certainly hadn't found anything particularly lacking in beauty on their journey so far, unless you counted Sumac the chicken. And they didn't need to *find* him; he kept finding *them*. They needed to get *rid* of him. He had a sudden thought.

"Hey, Vile, do you think Quinsy is what the oracle meant? About finding beauty in something ugly?" Twig rather liked the idea. It made him feel better about leaving Sir Thinly with the siren.

Vile considered it for a moment. "Doubtful. After all, it was Sir Thinly that found what he was looking for, not us. And, honestly, her singing's not really all that."

"Have you any message in *retuuuurrrrnnnn*?" interrupted Zinnia.

"Er, just tell her we're on Bone End investigating the disappearance of Prince Igneous of Rockpool. And that we're doing well."

"Liar," yawned Vile, settling deeper into her hammock.

Zinnia smiled at him and held out a hand. Twig dug out another sugar cube. "I bet Witch Wormwood already paid you, didn't she?"

The pixie just snatched the cube and disappeared

with a twinkly giggle.

They heard Beaky return in the middle of the night and settle himself into the crow's nest. Or, at least, Twig hoped it was Beaky, because it certainly was something very large. But he was too tired to worry about it much and the hammock was too comfortable. His head still felt a little fuzzy from his encounter with the siren and even Glimfinkle's snoring didn't annoy him for once. For a tiny little gnome, he really did have a prodigious snore.

* * *

They were awakened at the crack of dawn by an ear-piercing scream, a deep-throated bellow from above their heads, and the all-too-familiar sulphurous stink of rotten eggs. Twig promptly half-fell out of his hammock.

"Watch it!" yelled Glimfinkle, who had made his bed out of an old hat he'd found on the floor that hadn't smelled too horrible. "Gnome on the floor! Gnome on the floor!"

Vile helped untangle Twig. "Smells like the foul fowl

is back," she said in between yawns. "I don't know how he keeps managing to find us. I mean, how fast can a chicken fly?"

"He ain't a normal chicken, as ye well know," said Glimfinkle darkly, trying to be heard over a series of unnatural squawks and bellows. "Dunno why he can lay eggs, anyway. Shouldn't he be a cockerel and not a hen?"

"I did hit him with his gran's *Hen*bit curse," said Vile, shrugging. "If he'd been a normal person instead of a wizard, he'd probably be running around a farm right now eating worms instead of chasing us across the kingdoms. He's obviously still got some of his powers left. What kind of proper chicken lays rotten eggs, anyway?"

Twig peeked out of one of the portholes, but he couldn't see much because it had been egged by Sumac. Sticky, goopy, slightly green and mouldy-looking yolk dripped down the window. "We'd best get downstairs and do something," he said.

"Yeh," said Glimfinkle. "We don't want to get kicked out of the only inn on Bone End."

It was a scene of total chaos outside the Shin and Bone. Pegfoot was stomping around in a circle, waving an old pirate cutlass in the air and cussing a blue streak. Three of his former crew, still dressed in their pyjamas, were busy scrambling around trying to avoid the sharp edge of the blade and catch Sumac the chicken at the same time. Sumac, even more boil-ridden than the last time Twig had caught a glimpse of him, was flapping circles around them all while squawking and periodically bombing the confused ex-pirates with rotten eggs. Beaky flew above all of that, bellowing.

"Devil birds! We're bein' attacked by devil birds!" Pegfoot crowed at the top of his lungs.

"Gah! What *is* that smell?" wailed one of the pirates. He had a handlebar moustache that drooped down past his chin. He was wielding a fishing net with little success.

"Er, you should do something, Twig," said Vile, elbowing him as they stood in the doorway.

"What, exactly?" Maybe it was the abrupt awakening, but Twig had no ideas. Not one.

"Someone get me my fire lance!" Pegfoot jabbed

his cutlass in the air, very nearly poking Sumac, who laid another rotten egg in his surprise. It just missed the ex-pirate and splattered on the ground. But then Pegfoot's wooden foot stepped right on the gloppy mess and he skidded and slid into one of his mates.

"I got ya, Captain!"

But he didn't. They both went down, taking the handlebar moustache pirate along with them. There was so much flailing about that soon all three were tied up in the fishing net. The last crewman left standing only had a broomstick. He let out a wild yell and launched it into the air when he saw the state of his compatriots.

Except for Pegfoot, who was still yelling and, of course, blind, they all watched with bated breath as the broom flew into the air. Up, up, up it rose, showing a surprising accuracy. Right as it was about to whack Sumac the chicken, the foul bird squawked in wild-eyed fear, scrunched his neck down like he was concentrating particularly hard, and let loose with a flaming egg. He rocketed off into the air like a fireball until he was just a distant speck in the sky. The flaming egg fell to the ground and bounced until it rolled to a stop in front of Vile. She poked it with the toe of her boot and then stomped on it. It squished but didn't squelch.

"Hard-boiled," she said.

Beaky let out one last bellow and settled himself back on to the crow's nest. All was quiet, though smelly.

"Well," said Vile, "I guess that's how he travels so fast."

"Bloomin' bird's still got some magic left in him," said Glimfinkle from his perch on her shoulder.

"What's happened? What's going on? Where're the devil birds?" Pegfoot had noticed the lack of squawks and screeches, but his cutlass was still slashing about. He'd managed to get that arm through the net.

"Er, Pegfoot," said Twig, taking care to stay clear of the sword. "He's gone. That is, the chicken is gone. Well, he's not a chicken, exactly. He's actually a wizard, but he's currently a chicken. And he's disappeared."

"I got him!" The pirate that had thrown the broom was dancing a jig. "Me, Unlucky Pete, I got him! Blasted him clear out of the sky!"

Twig didn't bother to correct him. "And the other bird, he's with us, actually. But he's good. He's a magpie."

"I ain't never seen a magpie that big before," said Unlucky Pete. He bravely stepped forward and took hold of Pegfoot's wrist, stilling the waving cutlass. It looked like he'd done it before.

"He's. . ." Twig wasn't sure how to explain it.

"Boy wizard here magicked Beaky," said Glimfinkle, "so's sometimes he's a regular magpie and sometimes he's a bloomin' boobrie."

"We're *really* sorry about the mess," said Twig. "And all the fuss. We'll clean it all up."

> "With this wink,
> Get rid of the stink."

He cast the spell and winked. The nasty sulphur smell disappeared with a *poof.*

Pegfoot took a big sniff. "Oh, aye, that's better, lad. Porkbelly, get me out of this net, would you?"

"I'm in it too, Captain," said the one with the handlebar moustache.

"Ah, that you are," said Pegfoot. "I couldn't smell you

before with that rotten stink."

Twig and Vile helped Unlucky Pete untangle Pegfoot, Porkbelly and the last crew member, Beefstew, who had been (and still was) the Shin and Bone's cook. He was also Porkbelly's younger brother. By the time they were all out and the last of the eggs and feathers were swept away, the sun was well up and more than one tummy was rumbling in hunger.

"We'll pack our stuff up and get on our way," said Twig. "Again, I'm really sorry about everything. Sumac won't bother you again. He's just after us. If we go, he'll follow." Even the thought of it made his shoulders slump. Bone End was a windy place. Maybe he could magic up a decent shelter out of rocks?

"What're you on about, boy?" Pegfoot clapped him on the back and stumped off in the general direction of the Shin and Bone. Porkbelly gently prodded him to set him on the right course. "That's the best time I've had in an ogre's age! And now that we know what we're up against, me and the lads can have some real fun!" Pegfoot clapped his hands together. "Right, boys?"

The ex-pirates all cheered. "Now, then," said

Beefstew, tying his apron tight, "who's wanting breakfast?"

"Me!" said Glimfinkle. "So long as it's not eggs."

10

IN WHICH THERE IS A TOWER

After breakfast, Twig and Glimfinkle flew towards the Kraken's Toothpick on Beaky. He was only of a size to carry the two of them, even after Beefstew's hearty breakfast (which had consisted entirely of different types of slightly fishy sausages and thick slabs of bread and no eggs). Vile had volunteered to stay behind, saying she had something to do anyway.

The Kraken's Toothpick stood out as the tallest thing around for miles and miles. Knucklebone Cliff was the highest point on Bone End and the tower was at the very top of that. It had *probably* not been built by the gigantic sea monster it was named after, though it was hard to imagine who or what else would have been able to put it there. It was made out of the masts of countless ships: big ones, little ones, and ones that had definitely been destroyed by something that left behind really big bite marks.

As they approached, Twig could see that it wasn't just a tower. Or, at least, not a normal tower like the one that he'd lived in with Ripplemintz the Sage. Besides the fact that it was made out of masts, the bottom of the building was like a bloated beast, expanding out in every direction. If anything, it looked more like an octopus with knobbly short tentacles, wearing a really, really tall and pointy hat. There were a lot of porthole-shaped windows but only one door was visible, more or less in the centre of the belly of the beast.

After circling it a few times, Glimfinkle had Beaky land behind some boulders not too far from the tower, just off the path. There weren't any trees to provide cover, so it was the best they could do. Rocks of all shapes and sizes dotted the area and there were some large rosemary bushes, but that was it. Bone End really

was a barren place.

"Wot do ye think?"

"I don't know," said Twig. "I didn't see anyone in any of the windows, but Beaky was flying awfully fast. How about you?"

Before Glimfinkle could say anything, Beaky nudged him with his huge head and knocked the gnome over.

"Hey! Wot was that for, ye feathery beast?"

Beaky *humphed* softly and nudged the gnome again, finally rolling him to a spot where he could see the path beyond the boulder. Glimfinkle took one look and then scampered back to Twig. Beaky backed into the shadow of the rock and squatted down, until all you could really make out of him was the gleam of his yellow, saucer-shaped eyes. When he closed them, he disappeared completely.

"Quick! Hide! Somebody's comin'! We're jus' supposed to be reconnoitrin' fer now, ain't we?"

"Hide where?" Twig looked around. Anyone coming down the path would be sure to see him, and if he made a run for it, the ground was littered with pebbles that would make too much noise.

"Well, *I* don't know!" Glimfinkle pulled his pointy red hat off and crouched down behind a rock. "Use yer magic or yer head, one of 'em!"

"Um . . . oh. . ." Twig squeezed his eyes shut. He had to do something, fast. He whispered a spell.

> *"It's me*
> *You can't see.*
> *So walk on by,*
> *Don't be shy."*

He felt the familiar sizzle of his magic sparkle around him. He opened his eyes. Had it worked? He looked down. Oh, no. He could still see himself. He got down on his knees and whispered to Glimfinkle, "Can you see me?"

The gnome peered up at him. "Are ye daft? Ye look the same as ye always look."

Twig stood back up. Should he try and run for it then? Just brazen it out? Crouch down behind the boulder and hope for the best? Jump on to Beaky's back and fly away? He twitched, first looking one way and then the other. What should he *do*?

But then it was too late. He heard the unmistakable *jingle clank* of a knight's footsteps and a moment later the knight himself strode into view.

This knight was in better shape all round than Sir Thinly. From his surcoat, Twig could see that he was from the rich kingdom of Aramore, though he only knew *that* because their coat of arms had been all over the Euphonium. Aramore was where the wizard Pumice Pummelstone was from. A knight from there was bound to be well-off. In fact, the knight's armour was so shiny and undented that it looked brand new. He was reading a parchment and mumbling to himself something about his horse throwing a shoe as he walked.

"Er, hello," said Twig.

The knight, startled, looked up and right at him. "Who said that?" He dropped what he'd been reading and drew his sword. Then he turned in a slow circle with his sword held at the ready. "Who goes there?"

Twig was about to repeat his greeting when

Glimfinkle poked him in the foot with his own toothpick of a sword. He couldn't help the "Ow!" that escaped him, but then he clamped his hand over his mouth. Maybe the knight couldn't see him after all!

"Is someone there? Show yourself!" The knight looked very nervous now and took a few swipes with his sword at thin air.

Twig waved his hands about and made silly faces when the knight turned back his way, but the knight didn't react at all. The spell *had* worked!

"I, Sir Moreton of Aramore, demand that you show yourself!" The knight's voice had gone a little high-pitched and wobbly. He took a step in Twig's direction, sword still at the ready. It looked very sharp.

It suddenly occurred to Twig that, just because the knight couldn't see him, that didn't mean he couldn't stab him. He might even poke him by accident! He took a step away from the knight, but that made some of the pebbles roll and clack against each other.

Sir Moreton took another, slightly more quivering step, in the direction of the noise. He waved his sword about in increasingly erratic circles. Twig looked at

Glimfinkle, still ducked down behind the small rock. The gnome looked back up at him and then rolled himself into an even tighter little ball like a roly-poly.

The knight was so close now that Twig would never be able to get another spell out without being heard and possibly skewered. Maybe making himself invisible hadn't been such a good idea. He probably could have talked his way out of it or even just explained himself. It's not like Sir Moreton was necessarily a *bad* knight.

But Sir Moreton was, at this point, a very *nervous* knight. "I say, I shall gut thee! The knights of Aramore do not take being ambushed lightly!" He was whipping the sword around quite wildly now. Twig sucked in a breath when the tip of it whistled past, only inches from his nose. What should he do?

He felt another sharp poke on his foot. Glimfinkle had stabbed him again. He looked down, taking care not to shift his feet and make any noise. The gnome mouthed "Get ready" and then let out a low warbling whistle. Beaky's huge eyes snapped open. With a raspy chatter from deep in his throat, he stood up and took a step forward.

Sir Moreton took one look at the giant black-feathered beast unfolding from the shadows and dropped his sword. Then he ran away down the path towards the tower as quickly as he could with a *clank, rattle, clank*. It wasn't actually a very fast run, but it was a very noisy one.

Glimfinkle stood up and stretched. "I bet he's gonna have to change his armour when he gets wherever he's goin'," said the gnome with a snigger.

Beaky gave the chortling bellow that Twig had learned was his version of a laugh. It was actually scarier than his normal roar. The sound of the clanking rattle of the retreating knight increased in speed.

Twig tried to pick up the sword. It was heavier than he expected and he almost fumbled it, but luckily Glimfinkle was still staring after the knight and didn't notice. The gnome would never have let him live it down. He carefully leaned the sword against the boulder and picked up the parchment the knight had dropped. It smelled of flowers and had a whiff of strange magic about it. It didn't feel wizardy or even witchy.

It was . . . a love letter . . . advert?

Beautiful Damsel in Distress
Seeks a Charming Prince or Brave Knight
to Lift my Curse with True Love's First Kiss.

I beg thee to come and rescue me from my captivity on the island of Bone End. Must be at least 178 centimetres tall. Second sons OK. Must have own horse.  *No wicked stepmothers or poison apples in the family tree. No half beasts, farm boys or trolls need apply. Must like toads.*

At the bottom was a map of Bone End with a big heart drawn around the Kraken's Toothpick.

Twig could feel whatever magic had been cast on the parchment tickling him like it was trying to worm its way in. He threw up a quick protection spell and the tingly feeling went away.

He bent down and showed the letter to Glimfinkle. "I think this is what's been drawing all those princes and knights and whatnot here," he said. "There was some kind of a spell or something cast on it. I could feel it, but it wasn't super strong."

"Prob'ly aimed at fancier fellows than ye from the sound of it," said the gnome. "Ye don't exactly qualify on any of the points, ye know."

"That's true. Do you think we'll be able to get into the tower like this? What if there's a spell or glamour of some kind on it? Whoever sent the letter has some kind of magic."

"There's only one sure way to find out," said Glimfinkle. "I think we've reconnoitred enough. Yer just goin' to have to become a prince."

IN WHICH THERE ARE A
LOT OF FROGS

While Twig was trying not to be skewered, Vile was on a quest of her own. Following the directions that Pegfoot had grudgingly given her, she found the Moaning (now Croaking) Cave a little after lunchtime. The mouth of the cave was off the beach not too far north from the end of the Seven Sisters, but she probably could have found it even without directions because of the spine-tingling sound it produced.

The Moaning Cave had always made a lot of noise with the constant breeze off the Deep Sea entering the mouth of the cave system and running deep into the land. It was a creepy, eerie sound, like a group of banshees had congregated together to have a good cry. But now, it sounded like those banshees had decided to have a group wail while stirring a massive vat of very angry frogs.

The wooden fence that Pegfoot and his mates had put up to keep the frogs in wasn't very tall, but then, frogs were very short. That hadn't stopped them from trying to escape, though. Vile climbed up and peeked over the makeshift fence to find dozens and dozens of frogs and toads of all shapes and sizes scrambling over

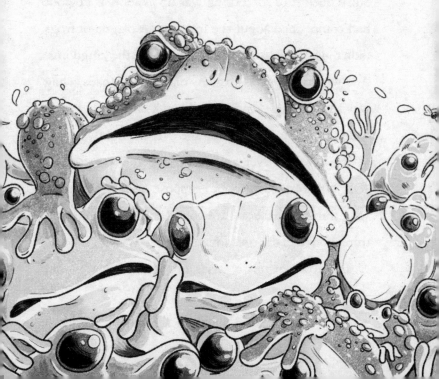

each other trying to find a way out. It was a squirmy green seething mass of angry amphibians.

"Oi! You, frogs!" yelled Vile. "Shut up a minute so I can think or I'll curse you again!"

All of the frogs except for one particularly warty toad snapped their mouths shut. That one hopped up on top of his green brothers in arms and let out a loud *crooooaaaakk* that was clearly neither intimidated nor scared. He had a yellow stripe down his back and his rear legs were oddly short and stubby. A natterjack.

"Hmmm," said Vile. "That's what I was afraid of." She'd been sure something was up as soon as Pegfoot had complained about the invasion. A plague of frogs didn't just show up for no reason, not in the kingdoms. And where there was an army of frogs and toads, a hag was sure to be behind it. She'd stake her dinner on it and that was not something she ever did lightly.

She reached over and picked up the angry toad. "OK, little Mr Bossy Boots. I suppose you're a wizard or something of that sort, are you? Looks to me like you think you're in charge, anyway."

The toad let out a series of increasingly agitated

croaks and *skree, skree, skree* scritchy scratches.

"Oh, you can stop yelling. I can't understand a word you're saying." She cocked her head at the toad, inspecting him thoroughly, top to bottom. She poked at a few of his warts, but when she tried to look inside his mouth, he nearly bit her.

"You want some more warts? I'll give you some. Don't think I won't." Vile shook a finger at him until he looked suitably bug-eyed and subdued. She sighed. "Look, I'm going to try and remove the curse, but I can't promise anything. It's hard to remove another hag's curse. And this one looks pretty strong, frankly. And kinda familiar." She had a bad feeling in her belly. It wasn't her hag sense this time, though, but common sense. Not many hags specialized in frogs and toads. She herself preferred to work in boils and inexplicably itchy noses. She saved transformations for people who especially deserved it, like evil wizards and shopkeepers that tried to stiff you.

Vile set the toad down at her feet. She dug in her bag to see what she had with her. It wasn't much. She mostly carried things to cast hexes and curses, not

133

break them. She'd have to wing it.

First, she took out some salt. "Hold still," she told the toad. "This'll sting your toes if you step in it." She sprinkled it around him in a circle as he eyed her distrustfully. Salt was good for protection, but also repelling things, especially warty, toady things. Maybe it would help.

Technically, she should be giving the toad a full-blown bath. And what she *really* needed were dragons' tears, the juice of seven limes and a sprinkle of rosemary, but dragons' tears weren't exactly easy to come by. Or she could try her great aunt Agrimony's favourite jinx-removing powder, which included her namesake agrimony, plus wisteria and hydrangea blossoms picked during a full moon.

Of course, Great Aunt Agrimony's hagging hadn't exactly been the best. She *had* been eaten by ogres, so obviously her protection charms had been rubbish.

Vile sprinkled some dried angelica and arrowroot powder on the toad's bulbous head. She took her right thumb and put it between her first two fingers and pointed it right at the toad. It blinked up at her. She stared down at it. Was it doing anything?

The toad fidgeted, one flat foot flopping into the salt. He started like he'd been stung by a bee and let out a mighty *skree, skree* that changed mid-croak to a startled "Ow, whoa, ow!"

Vile scooped him up. He was definitely still a toad, but a curly wisp of a beard had appeared on his chin, if you could say he had a chin at all.

"Oh, stop griping, it was just a bit of salt."

"It hurt!" The toad was about to say more when he came to the sudden realization that he wasn't croaking any more. "Hey, I can talk!" His voice was thin and reedy, but definitely human-ish. "What about the rest of me?" He also sounded imperious and aristocratic. Just her luck.

Vile looked away. "Well, I didn't have a lot of supplies with me. And, like I said, it's a pretty strong curse."

The toad blinked slowly, as if he were digesting a fly. "So, can you remove it, or not?"

Vile shifted on her feet. She could practically feel all the other frogs and toads leaning closer to listen. Not one was croaking or warbling. "Maybe."

135

A chorus of croaks arose.

"Quiet!" This time it was the toad yelling. The others settled down. "Let us begin again. I am Chert Boulderwort, Court Wizard of the Kingdom of Rockpool. Who, exactly, are you?"

"A hag, obviously. King Jasper sent us to look for Prince Igneous."

"Excellent, excellent. You said 'us'? So there are more of you?" Chert tried to cock his head to get a better look at her, but mostly succeeded in making himself look lopsided.

"Yeah. Me and Twig Thicket the wizard and ... Glimfinkle the gnome." She'd almost left off the gnome, but knew she'd never hear the end of it if she had and he caught wind of it.

"Twig Thicket? That name sounds familiar..." Chert gave an involuntary hop as it hit him. "Oh! The winner of the last Euphonium!"

That set the other frogs and toads to croaking again, but this time in excitement.

"But didn't he give all his magic away to Kudzu of the Spire?" The toad flicked his tongue out in annoyance.

"That's who King Jasper should have sent. Or Pumice Pummelstone, as much as I personally detest that show-off. Why did the king send a half-grown hag, a useless boy and . . . a *gnome*, of all things."

Vile poked the toad right in the nose. "OK, one, Twig's still got his magic. Two, I already told you I didn't have the right supplies with me. Three, if you insult me again, I'm perfectly happy to leave you all right here. Technically, the king just said to bring back Prince Igneous for the reward. He didn't say anything about *you*."

Chert let out a small *eep* that sounded half toad and half human. He dipped his large head in what was probably meant to be a bow. "My apologies, Ms. . .?"

"Hornwort. Vile Hornwort."

"H . . . Horn . . . Hornwort. . .?" The toad visibly shrank into himself.

Vile was pretty sure she knew why. "I see you've heard of us."

"Yes," said Chert carefully. "I do believe I've had the displeasure of meeting your older sister." He gave a mournful sigh. "I'm afraid I didn't see her true intentions until she told me her full name ... right before she transformed me and chucked me out of the Kraken's Toothpick like yesterday's soup."

Vile nodded. "I was afraid of that. Nasty always did have a thing for frogs and toads. You're lucky she didn't try to make you into toad soup after she transformed you."

IN WHICH THERE STILL
ISN'T A PRINCE

"How in the world am I supposed to become a prince?" asked Twig.

"Yer a wizard, figure it out," said Glimfinkle.

"I'm *not* transforming myself," said Twig. Every time he'd tried a transformation spell, either on purpose or not, it hadn't worked out well. Especially the time he and Vile had been stuck as mice and she'd almost been eaten by an owl. What if he tried to transform himself into a prince and got stuck as whatever he turned into? Not that being a prince *sounded* like it would be a bad thing, but his spells had a tendency to do the ...

unexpected. He wasn't about to cast anything big on himself without knowing what it was going to do. Not any more.

"Ye don't have to *be* a prince," said the gnome, kicking at Twig's foot. "Ye just have to *look* like one. And act like one, but all ye gotta do there is act like a fancy fop who thinks everythin' belongs to 'im. Easy peasy."

"Oh," said Twig. That made sense. Sort of. He'd never met a prince before, but he'd met a couple of kings and that definitely described King Mervyn.

Glimfinkle walked around Twig, looking him up and down. "Though, ye need a lot of work, lad. Best start on the clothes, I suppose. Ye look like the broke young travellin' hedge wizard ye are."

"Right," said Twig. That did seem the easiest bit to fix. He emptied out the contents of his sack to take a look at what he had to work with. Some of it had been given to him by Ripplemintz the Sage before he had left Muckwood, and he hadn't been able to bring himself to throw those bits out, even if they seemed awfully useless.

He had:

The bag of shells from the shellycoat he'd met in the Withering Swamp, though some had already been used for spells. Half a spool of thread. Two rusty iron nails. A bag of sugar cubes. A broken mousetrap, though he had already repurposed the long-dead mouse that had been stuck in it into clothes for Glimfinkle. A supply of dragon mint from Witch Wormwood. A few black feathers from Beaky (he wasn't even sure how those had wound up in his bag). A spare tunic given to him by an innkeeper that was big enough to fit both him and Vile at the same time. A flagon of water. A couple of interesting rocks he'd picked up along the way. And there was the sword that Sir Moreton had left behind.

It wasn't much.

He'd made his cloak mostly out of sky and cloud. Maybe he could use what he had and what was around him, though mainly that was rocks, sand and rosemary.

"To look like a prince,
I'll need to convince.
Make me some clothes

As fine as fine can be.

Even sand and rocks

Could make good trousers and socks."

A sparkle-filled gust of wind sprang up out of nowhere and surrounded him. Glimfinkle backed hastily away and hid behind a rock, but the wind grabbed that up too. The gnome dashed over to Beaky and clung on to his sturdy leg. Next, the spell picked up sand and Twig closed his eyes against the sting of it. He felt his body being tumbled this way and that with clicks and clacks, probably from the rocks.

When the spell was done, he opened his eyes and looked down at himself. He was wearing fine sand-coloured breeches and stockings that tucked neatly into a pair of boots, which looked like they were studded with flecks of gems. The innkeeper's plain brown tunic had been turned into a finely embroidered one that cinched neatly at his waist. It had a faint wisp of rosemary about the delicate stitches. He had a floppy hat on his head with a matching design, and his cloak of sky was now trimmed with something fluffy that he suspected had been made from Beaky's feathers, though thankfully it had been turned the green of rosemary instead of being left black.

"What do you think, Glimfinkle?"

The gnome let go of his tight hold on Beaky's leg and gave Twig another walk around. "Not bad, lad. Wouldn't mind me some boots like that, later. But yer still a scrawny git. More like a princeling than a prince."

Well, thought Twig, he *was* just not quite twelve. And he wasn't going to change that. What if he accidentally aged himself up and wasn't able to age himself back down? He didn't want to be *old*. Not yet.

"I'll try a glamour to *appear* older," he said. He thought for a minute, trying to be as specific in the spell as Ripplemintz had always advised him to be. Not that the sage had often heeded his own advice.

> *"To those in the Toothpick,*
> *That I want to trick,*
> *Make me look older*
> *And . . . bolder!"*

A shower of sparkles rained down upon him. "So, how's that?" he asked the gnome.

"How should I know?" said Glimfinkle. "I ain't in the tower. Ye look the same to me."

"Ah. Right." He cleared his throat. "Well, let's, er, go, I guess." He picked up everything from the ground, including the sword (first making it feather-light and smaller) and shoved it all in his sack. The spell had worked on his bag too; now it looked like leather with a golden trim.

"Me and Beaky'll keep watch from out here," said the gnome.

"What? You're not coming?"

The gnome winked at Twig. "Who's gonna run for help if we're stuck in there with ye? Besides, what would a prince be doin' with a boobrie and a gnome?"

Twig didn't like the idea of going in alone. Maybe he should have waited for Vile to be able to come? They could have fed Beaky some more food. But then, she'd be the one who Glimfinkle would have to run to for help if he needed it... He took a deep breath. It was OK. It wasn't like having a gnome in his pocket would actually be helpful. Glimfinkle could be called a lot of things, but *helpful* generally wasn't one of them.

"Just let out a yell or somethin' if you need us. Worst comes to worst, I can have Beaky do some gobblin'. We'll be circlin' up there." The gnome pointed up to the clear blue sky.

Beaky snapped his beak together with a crack.

"Right," said Twig again. "Then, uh, I'm off." He straightened his shoulders, threw them back and put his chin up. Be confident. Or, at least, look confident. He could do it.

He strode down the path, trying to walk like he remembered King Mervyn of Muckwood had. He felt like a stork, but he kept at it.

As he rounded the corner of a particularly large boulder, he got his first clear look at the Kraken's Toothpick. It was really big. And with the mismatched appearance of countless ship masts, driftwood and what looked a great deal like sun-bleached bones, it was about the furthest thing from a place you'd want to visit. Whatever damsel was stuck in it was sure to be in distress indeed. The few windows there were looked like they were staring down at him, but that was probably just because they were all round, like unblinking owl eyes.

He pulled the hat down low over his forehead and walked right up to the door. Unlike the rest of the Toothpick, the door looked relatively solid and new and was painted a deep, dark black. Another one of the flyers was tacked to the door. He could feel the faint tingle of magic coming from it, making him glad he'd shielded himself already. He stuck his chin up even higher and rapped smartly on the door.

Nothing happened.

He knocked again, a little harder. Nothing.

Should he just open it?

He knocked one more time, this time adding a spell push behind it. THUNK, THUNK. The door shook.

"Hold your horses!" The door flung open. Sir Moreton, looking slightly sweaty and dishevelled with his helm under his arm, stood there. His annoyed expression changed to one of surprise, mirrored by Twig. What kind of luck was it that the ONE knight he'd already met and cast a spell on was the one that

146

had opened the door? How could he explain that? If he cast a spell to make himself visible now, Sir Moreton would know for sure he was a wizard and not a prince.

"Who's there? Another suitor, I hope?" That was definitely a young woman's voice. It sounded bored but also strangely familiar, and not at all how Twig had thought a damsel in distress should sound.

"No one!" Sir Moreton stuck his head out and peeked first in one direction and then another. He took a step outside to get a better look. There was nothing for it. Twig would just have to sneak in. Maybe it was a blessing in disguise. The woman's voice had sounded far away, from somewhere up above. Maybe Sir Moreton was the only one at the door. Twig carefully squeezed by the knight and stepped inside. If he was lucky, he could get a good look around before anyone else noticed him.

The inside of the Toothpick smelled musty and stale. It was dark too, lit only by a few candles, and those were far away across the large, bare entryway. There were three doors leading in various directions but no windows. A rickety staircase was directly in front of him.

Creak. Someone was coming down the stairs. Someone with not-so-dainty footsteps. Someone who would be able to see him. Twig hesitated a moment and then crouched down into the dark, shadowy space under the stairs.

Creak. Thump. Creak. Thump.

Twig backed himself as far into the shadows as he could. A small but fairly filthy boot clunked on to the step in front of his nose, followed by another mismatched boot, just as dirty as the first. He could see the hem of a dress. Was *this* the damsel in distress? He held his breath.

Whoever it was finished clumping down the stairs and stood in the doorway, looking out at Sir Moreton, who was still turning this way and that and looking terribly confused. Long locks of brilliant, luxurious hair hung down the girl's back all the way to her knees.

As she turned to inspect Sir Moreton, Twig saw her face clearly in profile. A perfect button nose. Long eyelashes. Her clothes didn't go with her face at all. Her dress was patched and stained and she had a number of small leather pouches tied to her belt, much like the ones Vile carried in her bag at all times. In fact, there was something very familiar about the way the girl slouched and the way she put her hands on her hips.

"I swear, m'lady, I did hear the door!"

The girl turned back inside and Twig got his first really good look at her face. He had the niggling feeling that he had seen this girl somewhere before, but where? He'd never seen anyone this pretty, unless you counted Queen Coral. Was this girl half siren too? That might explain the magic he'd felt on the letter. But, no, it didn't seem like her boots were hiding any bird feet.

Then the girl grinned. A nasty, conniving grin. A twisty, not-very-nice grin. And Twig knew for certain exactly where he knew her from. It wasn't a smile you could forget.

13

IN WHICH TWIG DISCOVERS SOMETHING NASTY

Nasturtium "Nasty" Hornwort, the older sister Vile had cursed with beauty at the Euphonium hag scrap, let the door swing shut on Sir Moreton's foot as he tried to come back into the tower. She smiled in satisfaction at his grunt of pain. Twig repressed a shudder. It was definitely Nasty.

"Go have a look around outside. Maybe I'll let you back in later, if I feel like it." She clumped off back up the stairs. A bit of mud from one of her boots fell off on to Twig's head.

Twig rocked back on his heels. Now what? Would

Nasty recognize him in his princely disguise? They hadn't spent much time together – though, to be honest, any time spent with her was too much – but should he chance following her up the stairs? What was she even doing here? Why was she pretending to be a damsel in distress when she was the one who put people *in* distress? Was Prince Igneous above? What was she up to?

He brushed the dirt from his hair, climbed out from under the stairs and took a deep breath. He had to at least see if the prince was safe. Besides, he was wearing the fanciest clothes he'd ever worn. And the invisibility spell had worked, so his disguise spell should too. He could do this.

He took a deep breath and walked slowly up the stairs, with that stiff-legged stork walk that reminded him of King Mervyn. It was harder to do going up stairs, but he managed.

Creak. Shuffle. Creak. Shuffle.

The landing was a hallway with four doors and another set of stairs that went up again. Peering up the steps, he could see that the building narrowed from the next floor up and the stairs kept going on and on in a spiral, presumably to the very top of the Kraken's Toothpick. He could hear Nasty's footsteps continuing on up, but she wasn't the reason he was here. He needed to find the prince.

Three of the doors were closed and covered in cobwebs. The fourth, the furthest down the hall, was cracked open and he could see a flicker of firelight coming through and hear voices. He stork-walked that way, trying to hold his head high and his nose up. He imagined Vile telling him to look like he'd smelled something he didn't like. He took a haughty sniff and pushed the door open.

The room was absolutely packed full of a random collection of chairs, settees, footstools and even puffy floor pillows, mostly threadbare and old. And each seat held a bored-looking knight or prince and a few disgruntled (and less well-dressed) lower nobility, plus one brawny fellow unashamedly wearing a blacksmith's apron and sitting right by the fireplace. And each and every one of them all turned to look at him as the door *creeeeaaaakkkkeeeed* open.

"Er, hello," said Twig, completely forgetting to try and sound impressive. There were so many of them. Perhaps he should have expected that. Pegfoot had said there had been lots of nobility traipsing through Kneecap. He recognized a few knights from the queue at Coquina Castle. They must have been caught by the flyer on the door.

"Oh, lovely, *another* one," said a very well-dressed prince decked out in furs and a gold circlet, which seemed excessive even among this group. He had a long, thin nose which he used to great effect to look down at Twig with. "And from a poor kingdom, I wager, from the state of him."

"Do be so kind as to shut up, Prince Darrold," said an equally tall and thin prince wearing the familiar maroon and gold colours of Aramore, as were two other princes lounging next to him. "Wherever this little lordling is from is bound to be more civilized than Bragmore."

"Though no kingdom compares to Aramore, brother!" The smallest of the three matching princes said in a rush, but at least it was with a smile and nod

at Twig. "Well met, whoever you are, young lordling! I am Prince Dash of Aramore. And here are my brothers, Ash and Bash!"

"No Prince Cash?" asked Twig, unable to stop himself.

There was an uncomfortable silence in the room. All of the various princes and knights looked at each other and then at the floor.

"Prince Cash of Aramore was ... rejected by Lady Nasturtium," said a knight, wearing a surcoat that proclaimed him to be from the faraway northern kingdom of Justice. His voice had a ring to it, like he was used to making himself heard.

"*Lady* Nasturtium?" Twig nearly choked.

"Oh, have you not yet met our lady?" This was from another knight, who clasped his hands together and sighed, making a sappy expression that did not at all look at home on his scarred face. "You're in for a treat. Not only a vision to behold, but so kind and lovely as well!"

"Er, right," said Twig. He looked around the room at a bunch of nodding faces, all of them shining with excitement. A few were blushing. They were *definitely* under a spell of some kind. Nasty? Kind and lovely? Well, technically she *was* pretty now. But she still seemed all kinds of ugly on the inside, and that was what counted.

He took another good look around. The quicker he found Prince Igneous, the better. But he didn't see anyone that fit the description of a large, blocky prince, other than the one that looked like a blacksmith. He was a large, square-shouldered man. Twig walked over to him. The rest of the princes and knights and whatnot had started talking amongst themselves about the beauty of Lady Nasturtium and seemed to have forgotten him completely.

"Hi," he said to the blacksmith, holding out a hand. "I'm Twig."

"Greetings, Sir Twig. Or is it lord?" The man took his hand and shook it, completely engulfing Twig's in his own. He had hands as big as an ogre and nearly as hairy. "I am Stab, the blacksmith of Kneecap."

"Oh, I'm not a Sir," whispered Twig, relaxing. Somehow a blacksmith seemed a lot less threatening to talk to. "You can just call me Twig."

The blacksmith seemed to relax a little. "Well met, then. I must admit I am glad to see a fellow commoner here." Stab gave a pointed look in Prince Darrold's direction.

"Er, *why* are you here? No offence intended." Did that mean the spell on the advert worked on people who didn't meet the qualifications too? He was glad he'd blocked whatever it was. Maybe it was like a curse. Actually, that would make sense, considering it was Nasty who had cast it. Of course it was a curse.

"None taken," said Stab. "The lady had hired me for some work on—"

"You do know she's not an actual lady, right?" Twig interrupted, leaning forward so only Stab could hear him.

"Isn't she?" The blacksmith looked surprised. He shook his head. "Well, not that it matters to me." He blushed, twin roses on his round cheeks. "Perhaps, then, that would work in my favour..."

Twig leaned even closer. He wondered if he could snap Stab out of his strange attraction. If he could, then maybe he could do the same for the princes. "To tell you the truth, she's actually a . . . hag."

Stab lumbered to his feet, knocking over a coal scuttle next to the fireplace with a loud clatter. Lumps of coal scattered everywhere. "Shut your mouth and call me Rose Red!"

The others in the room looked over at the mess. "Oh, what is it now, blacksmith?" asked a foppish lord wearing the muddy brown and orange colours of Dunmire. He looked like a melted dumpling.

Stab pointed dramatically, right at Twig, his thick finger almost touching Twig's nose. "This little one says that our lady is . . . is a . . . is a . . . HAG!"

There was a loud almost-sighing sound as a collective breath was drawn in by everyone in the room, including Twig. Then there was a loud scraping of chairs against the wooden floor as the assorted princes, knights and lesser-ranked but equally affronted nobility all stood up at once.

"How DARE he?!"

Twig wasn't even sure who it was that yelled the first "Get him!" and he didn't waste time trying to argue. He'd always found nobility a bit intimidating, and having them all rush him at once with wild eyes and whatever sharp, pointy objects they had about them was enough to convince him he'd been right. He ran for the window closest to him and burst through it, yelling a simple but powerful one-word spell as he fell – *"Fly!"*

14

IN WHICH TWIG FLIES

Twig had flown any number of times on Beaky's back, but it was an entirely different proposition when you were doing the flying yourself and you didn't have wings or a clue as to what you were doing.

The window he'd launched himself through overlooked the coast, which meant he found himself suddenly hurtling down the side of Knucklebone Cliff towards certain doom. Certain doom, of course, meaning rocky shoals and the bottomless depths of the Deep Sea full of the kind of sea monsters that would chew your leg off as soon as they saw you. If you survived the fall.

The spell took hold of him with a *zing* like lightning. He stopped falling immediately, which was a very good thing. For one calm, quiet moment, he hung suspended in the air, but then he fell into a jerky, uncontrolled flight, arms and legs akimbo, his robe fluttering and flapping over his head, which wasn't as good. Seeing as how the cape was made of mostly cloud and sky, it seemed almost at home, but it was the only part of him that did.

The stark face of the rocky cliff was coming at him awfully fast. Twig tried flapping his arms and legs like he was swimming in the air, but only managed to flop himself over so that he was upside down and couldn't see where he was going any more.

"What're ye doing, ye daft wizard?" Glimfinkle, still riding on Beaky, had swooped down to fly next to him.

"Trying to fly!" yelled Twig. The words whipped away in the wind. He flapped his arms and legs harder. He spun in the air like a top. His stomach was not at all happy with this new development. He couldn't see a thing, just a blur of white and blue and grey.

Beaky let out a chirruping bellow.

"Put yer legs together like a rudder!" Glimfinkle translated for Twig. "And stop thrashin' about like a fledglin'!"

Twig did as he was told. He pressed his legs together and pointed his toes, trying to imagine what a bird's tail feathers looked like when they were flying. He straightened his arms, trying to imitate what Beaky's wings did when the magpie was gliding, cupping his palms to try and hold the air. Both things helped; he was soon right-side up again and not spinning. His stomach settled back into roughly the place it was supposed to be, but his breakfast felt like it was still sloshing around.

Now he was sort of gliding along the face of Knucklebone Cliff. He took a deep, gulping breath and let it out in a *whoosh* of relief. Then wished he hadn't, when he saw where he was headed.

There was a very large rock outcropping, jutting directly into his path. Beaky let out a screech that made all the nesting seagulls take off into the air at once in a flurry of white and grey feathers.

"Ye need to bank and turn!" Glimfinkle was

screaming at the top of his lungs.

"How?!" Twig ducked his head as a startled seagull flew right by him.

He needed wings. Fast. An image of himself walking around with wings instead of arms flashed in Twig's head. No! He had to think of something better. He didn't want to transform himself into some weird siren hybrid.

> *"May my cape*
> *Take shape!*
> *Let me fly*
> *Through the sky!"*

He reached back with both hands, grabbed hold of the edges of his cloak of sky and cloud and stretched his arms out wide. He flapped the arm closest to the cliff, breathing a sigh of relief as the cloak held and caught air. He kept flapping as he took a sharp turn away from the cliff and out towards the open sea.

"Now yer using yer head, boy!" Glimfinkle said and then let out a squawk. The seagulls screeched back at the gnome and a contingent of them flew into formation in front of Twig. "Watch their wings and do what they do," said Glimfinkle. "They're no better'n sea rats, but they know how to fly!"

Twig followed the seagulls, trying to move his arms to mimic their wings. It was hard work, but now that he wasn't in imminent danger of splatting into the cliff, it suddenly hit him that he was *actually flying*. He let out a whoop and the seagulls answered him back with a call that sounded almost like they were laughing.

* * *

The seagulls led them all the way back to the Shin and Bone. Twig had a bit of a feel for flying by the time they reached the inn. It wasn't about big movements, but small ones. He carefully flapped his arms, keeping a tight hold on the edges of his cape. He spiralled closer and closer to the ground until, on the last loop, he relaxed and let his legs drop down. His feet touched the ground, toes first. He dropped his cloak and ran a few more steps on his toes before collapsing in a heap right outside the door of the inn. Glimfinkle and Beaky landed a bit more gracefully near to him. His arms ached like never before and his stomach was pretty sure he was still in the air. Flying was definitely not easy.

Vile flung open the door of the inn with a bang and ran out, not even looking surprised at seeing him in a pile on the ground.

"Vile," Twig yelled, "it's your sister!" at the exact same time as Vile shrieked, "Twig, it's Nasty!"

They stopped and looked at each other and then both spoke at the same time again: "How did you know?"

"What's nasty?" interrupted Glimfinkle.

"The damsel in distress," said Twig. "The one in the Kraken's Toothpick. She's no damsel. She's a hag! It's Vile's sister, Nasty." He turned to Vile. "But how did *you* know?"

Before Vile could say anything, a toad hopped

through the door and right up to Twig. "I suppose *this* is the great wizard Twig Thicket you were telling me about?"

"Uh, that's a talking toad," said Twig.

"I am Chert Boulderwort." The toad did a funny little bow that made him look like he was about to jump but had forgotten how. "Court wizard of Rockpool, at your service."

"Now I've seen everythin'," said Glimfinkle.

Beaky brought his head down and put his great big yellow eye up to the toad to get a closer look. Chert tried to hop backwards and wound up flat on his back instead, his legs kicking at the air. "I say! Call off your beast!"

"Beaky's no beast! You watch your little toady tongue!" Glimfinkle slid down Beaky's side and all the way along his leg to the ground. He stomped over to

Chert. "I've half a mind to let him eat you. He's probably never had

toad before."

Chert let out a squeak and flopped about on his back. "And you must be the gnome!"

"Obviously," said Glimfinkle, though he looked a little mollified at being recognized.

"Everyone shut it!" Vile stood, hands on her hips. "Or I'll turn you all into toads!"

There was a moment of silence. "I'm already a toad," said Chert finally. He managed to flop himself back around and tucked his legs underneath him.

"What's going on?" asked Twig.

"Nasty's handiwork," said Vile. "She prefers to work in amphibians. Green's her favourite colour."

That seemed to be their cue. The rest of the army of frogs and toads came hopping out of the Shin and Bone, ribbiting and croaking.

"Er," said Twig, as the horde surrounded him, "exactly how many of them are there? And who are they?" He picked up a small tree frog and brought it up to his face. "What's your name, little guy?"

The tiny green frog opened his mouth wide and croaked.

"I do believe that is Prince Cash of Aramore," said Chert. "But I could be wrong. I was busy being turned into a toad at the time."

"Oh," said Twig. "I, er, met your brothers."

The little frog gave a tiny leap and blinked at him.

"Well," said Glimfinkle, "this's a fine kettle o' fish, fer sure."

"Frogs, you mean," said Beefstew, coming to the door in his apron. He was brandishing a ladle. "You sure they're all actually people? I could use some legs for the soup."

There was a wild scramble as the army of frogs and toads scattered away from the cook, most of them winding up on Twig. They felt cool and slightly damp and squidgy.

"Quite certain, my good man," said Chert, though he too hopped closer to Twig. "And hopefully we will be restored to our former selves quickly." Beefstew shrugged and went back inside, humming to himself.

About sixty pairs of very hopeful unblinking bulbous eyes all turned to Twig.

IN WHICH THINGS
ARE HOPPING

"Er, why are all of them looking at me?" Twig set the frog that was possibly Prince Cash on the ground and prodded him with a finger until the little frog hopped away. He plucked another couple of frogs from his leg and set them down too. They immediately hopped back on. They were surprisingly sticky.

"Why, you won the Euphonium, didn't you?" Chert crept closer. "Certainly, you can remove a simple hag curse."

"Do *you* know how to remove a hag spell?" He didn't remember meeting Chert at the Euphonium, but as Twig was the youngest wizard to ever compete in the yearly wizard duel, that meant Chert *had* to be older and more experienced than he was.

"Well, no," said the toad. "My speciality is in metal dowsing." He cleared his throat with a croak. "If you need to find some silver or copper, I'm your wizard. I'm also excellent at making hourglasses. No one can make sand run like I can."

"Right," said Twig. Neither of those things sounded very useful for de-frogging.

Vile snorted. "A wizard shouldn't mess with a hag curse," she said. "Everyone knows that."

"Why?" asked Twig.

"You'll only make it worse," she said, crossing her arms.

"*You* were only able to give me my voice back," said Chert. "I trust a wizard over a hag any day."

"I *told* you I didn't have the right ingredients," said Vile. "And I asked Beefstew and he's got no idea where to get dragons' tears, much less the barrel of it we'd need to treat this many. And there's no Pixie Post box in Kneecap either. They're serious about their privacy here. So either you have to wait until we get back to the mainland, find a really depressed dragon, or get the hag that cursed you to remove it." She grimaced. "And Nasty'll never do that, so you're just gonna have to wait."

There was a shuffling of frog feet and some grumpy croaks.

"That is not acceptable," said Chert. His tiny beard quivered.

"Oh, let the lad try," said Glimfinkle, "after all, they're already frogs. It can't get much worse, can it?"

That was the type of thing one should never say in the kingdoms. Twig could think of a lot of things that could be worse than being a frog. Like being an exploded frog. A frog pancake. A toadstool.

"Whatever floats your warts," said Vile. "But don't blame me when things go wrong."

"Didn't you say he was the greatest wizard in all the kingdoms?" Chert absent-mindedly flicked his tongue out to grab a slug that had wandered near him. Then he realized what he had done and spat it back out. "Ugh!" He tried to rid himself of the taste but only managed to sputter. "I'm willing to take the risk. I never want to see another slug or fly or bug in my life!"

There was another round of croaks and ribbits, obviously in agreement.

"Er, I'll try," said Twig. "But I can't promise anything." He shakily stood up, dislodging the frogs and toads as gently as he could. His legs and arms still felt like jelly from his flying experience.

Vile took three very large steps backwards away from him. Twig gave her a look. She wasn't instilling him with confidence. She grinned and gave him a thumbs up, but that didn't make him feel any better either. He'd seen that grin before. She fully expected him to mess up. But he had to try. You couldn't succeed without trying. That was one of the few useful things that Ripplemintz had taught him.

He sighed. "Do I have a volunteer?"

The little tree frog that might have been Prince Cash of Aramore leapt into the air, bounced off the head of a larger toad, and landed in front of Twig.

"OK," said Twig. "Maybe everyone else should back up. You know, just in case." He tried not to look at Vile,

172

certain she was still grinning at him. Sometimes, she looked a lot like her sister.

The rest of the frogs and toads, other than Chert Boulderwort, obediently moved back until Twig was surrounded by a circle of anxious amphibians. Glimfinkle and Beaky went to stand by Vile. The gnome was grinning too. That *definitely* didn't make Twig feel any better. Or the fact that Beaky was eyeing the frogs quite hungrily. Maybe he should hurry or there wouldn't be anyone left to transform.

> *"What a strange*
> *Change.*
> *Let's fix*
> *The hag's tricks!"*

A shower of sparks flew from Twig's fingertips to land on the tiny frog waiting patiently in front of him. At first everything seemed to be going really well. The glittery sparks surrounded the frog, almost like he had been covered in frosting. Then the spell picked up his tiny body and spun him in the air like he was doing a pirouette in some kind of frog ballet, much like the spell that had given Twig his new clothes. But then, instead of growing larger, the already small frog began to shrink.

Smaller, smaller, smaller... Twig could only watch in horror. Had he just made a prince disappear? What did they do to you when that happened? But right before he thought the prince was gone for ever, the sparks *poofed* away in a puff of foul-smelling black smoke and a noise that sounded a great deal like a laugh. Like the kind of laugh a hag might give. It sounded exactly like Nasty.

All that was left was ... a small housefly buzzing around in circles in confusion.

Vile laughed so hard that she had to clutch her stomach and lean against Beaky. "I told you," she spluttered in between gasps of laughter. "You should know by now not to mess with a hag!"

"It's not funny!" Twig slapped a hand to his forehead. This was bad. So bad. He *had* made it worse. Being a fly was definitely a step below being a frog. It was only slightly better than being a slug. He sighed.

He'd never be able to show his face in Aramore again.

But then it got even worse.

As Prince Cash buzzed around confusedly, the onlooking circle of frogs and toads were mesmerized. Their bulging eyes were following his every move as if they couldn't help it. Twig only noticed when Chert, already the closest, took a sudden bumpy, ungainly run towards them on his stumpy little legs. His long tongue flicked out – *snap*! – and the fly was gone.

"Hey!" Twig grabbed Chert and smacked him on the back. "Spit him out!"

Chert's eyes bulged out even more, but after a few more pats, he hawked up a very toad-spit-covered fly. "Sorry, sorry," he said. "Don't know what came over me there. Couldn't quite help myself."

Twig set him down and gingerly picked up the bedraggled fly. Was he still alive? It wasn't like he could check for a pulse on a fly. He blew gently on the fly on his palm, trying to ignore how disgusting toad spit felt. It was gooey.

"Is the poor lad alive?" Chert at least sounded contrite.

Twig peered closer and blew another breath on to

Prince Cash. He was happy to see an answering flutter of wings. The fly used his two front legs to try and wipe some of the goo off. Twig gave a shudder. He couldn't even imagine how it felt to be bathed in toad spit. Or to be a fly, for that matter.

"I'm so sorry about that," he said. "I guess Vile was right. A wizard shouldn't mess about with hag magic."

"Ooooh," said Vile, almost chirping in glee, "someone write that down, will you? *Vile was right.*"

"Oh, shut up," said Twig. "That's not helpful. What do I do now?"

"Same thing as I said before," said Vile. "Either wait until we get back to the mainland and can get what we need or talk Nasty into removing her curse." She grinned again, completely ignoring the glares from scores of bulbous eyes. "And I can tell you which one is more likely to happen. . ."

"Best solve this Nasty problem soon," said Glimfinkle. "I don't think yer goin' to be able to keep yon herd from eating the fly prince for long."

Twig sighed again. Well, at least he could do something about that. He cast a spell to make a large glass containment bottle out of some of the nearby sand. At least there was an abundance of that on Bone End. He put in some sticks so it wasn't empty and carefully dropped the still damp fly into the bottle, leaving the top open so the poor prince could breathe. "We'll just keep him somewhere safe for now," he said and shuffled into the Shin and Bone, followed by a trail of frogs and toads.

* * *

They sat down for a supper of soup with Pegfoot and the ex-pirates. It featured a lot of carrots and potatoes and no frogs' legs, which was more than fine with everyone other than Beefstew. The bottle with Prince Cash in it was put up on a high shelf to keep it away from the other transformed princes and knights. Beefstew had even dropped some sugar water in the bottle for the fly to drink. They'd worked together to shoo the rest of the frogs and toads back into the garden, where they were making short work of whatever snails, slugs and bugs they could find. Even Chert was out there, though they heard him go "Blegh!" after every swallow.

"So, let me get this straight," said Pegfoot, waving a spoon in the air and nearly poking Porkbelly in the eye. "The lady up the Kraken's Toothpick, who's been attracting all manner of lovesick fools, is actually a cursed hag?"

"Yes," said Twig.

"And she's your sister?" He unerringly swivelled to point a finger directly at Vile's forehead.

"Yep," said Vile, sounding entirely too cheerful.

"And she's the one wot cursed her, too," said Glimfinkle, dunking a large crumb of bread into his tiny bowl. "A sort-of Rapunzel curse."

"Yer family sounds like mine," said Unlucky Pete rather mournfully as he absent-mindedly stirred his soup. "Me brother's the one what tried to get me hung for pirating."

"So why's she collecting all these princes and knights and turning 'em into frogs and toads anyway?" Porkbelly scratched his head with his spoon. "Not that hags have to make sense, mind, but seems a lot of trouble to go to."

"She's trying to break the curse," said Vile. "One of

the few ways to break it is with true love's first kiss. But Chert said that if anyone annoys her, she turns them into a frog." She slurped her soup. "Nasty always did like frogs and she's very easy to annoy."

"Why don't you just remove the curse on your sister?" asked Beefstew.

Vile shook her head emphatically no. "Not on your life," she said.

"But, Vile, that'd solve everything!" said Twig. "Well, not everything, but at least some of the things! If she's not cursed any more, she won't need all the princes and knights. Maybe the spell they're under will break if they see that she's not, you know, actually a beautiful damsel in distress and—"

"Nope. She deserves every second of misery after what she's put me through all my life." Vile raised her spoon in the air as if to emphasize the point. "Besides, it's about time she learned that what you look like isn't the important thing."

Pegfoot let out a thoughtful *humph*. "What exactly was it you cursed her with?"

"Beauty," said Vile. This time there was no

179

concealing her satisfied smile, not even the bit of carrot stuck in her teeth.

All of the pirates were silent for a long moment. "Beauty, you say?" asked Porkbelly.

"She's got hair like Rapunzel and eyes like Rose Red," said Twig, before he could stop himself. He blushed. "But she's still nasty as ... well, Nasty." He cleared his throat and snuck a peek at Vile. "You didn't change her personality any. She obviously hasn't learned anything from you cursing her."

Vile squinted at him. "Well, her attitude is what got her into this mess and it'll be the thing that keeps her in it too. Who'd fall in love with her?"

"How pretty are we talking, exactly?" That was Beefstew, who had leaned so far over the table that his beard fell into his soup.

"Not that pretty," said Twig, very carefully, looking at his supper and not at Vile.

"But yer sayin' that's where Stab the blacksmith disappeared off to?" Porkbelly shook his head. "Never known him to lose his head over a girl before."

"Might have to get a look at her meself," said

Unlucky Pete.

"I wouldn't recommend it," said Twig darkly. "You don't want to wind up like Stab or any of the others. I mean, Vile, what about all of them? It's not *their* fault they've been bamboozled. Or, you know, turned into frogs! Just remove Nasty's curse already!"

"Why?" asked Vile. "Why should I help them? What have they done for me? I bet most of them wouldn't even give me a crust of bread if I was starving."

Twig stared at her, open-mouthed. He wanted to argue, but he'd met Prince Darrold and suspected that he probably *wouldn't* help a beggar. But that wasn't an excuse. He needed to make Vile understand. Two wrongs didn't make a right. He had to think of something to convince her and Vile was just about as stubborn as Nasty was nasty. And hags lived by a whole other code that he still didn't understand.

As if it could tell what was going on in his head, the fly up on the shelf buzzed as loudly as a fly could buzz, flying around in agitated circles.

16

IN WHICH
PREPARATIONS ARE MADE

They all slept well that night, even Twig, though he almost fell out of his hammock a few times because he kept dreaming he was flying. Or maybe it was falling. He wasn't entirely sure because they felt very similar as far as his tummy was concerned, and he was too tired to really think about it or of ways to talk Vile into doing the right thing.

In fact, he was so tired he probably would have slept through breakfast if it hadn't been for the rousing shouts of a sea shanty from outside that woke him once the sun was up.

"Heave, ho! Away we go!
Raise it up higher, boys!

Pack the powder,
Stow the gear!
Show 'em we've got no fear!

Heave, ho! Away we go!
Mind the cannons, boys!"

Vile groaned and rolled out of her hammock. "What're those barmy pirates up to?" She opened one of the windows and looked out. Her eyes grew wide. "Oi! Come and see, Twig!"

Twig wiped the sleep out of his eyes and joined her at one of the portholes. The outside of the Shin and Bone was being transformed right in front of their eyes under Pegfoot's supervision. The one-legged pirate stood off to the side leading the chant at the top of his lungs, though he *was* facing out to sea rather than towards the inn. Even so, he seemed to know exactly where all of his men were at all times, interrupting his

183

singing to give them direction, and was quick to tell off Beefstew whenever the cook stopped to take a break.

"Lemme see too!" Glimfinkle tugged on Twig's trouser leg.

"I think we'd best go outside and see what they're up to," said Twig, scooping up the gnome on his way out. He wasn't sure he could believe his eyes.

But when he went outside, it was even stranger than he'd thought. The Shin and Bone had looked like a broken down, landlocked pirate ship before, but now it bristled spikes and poles with netting and rickety ladders that climbed up to the sky. It looked like a very large and dangerous hedgehog.

Some of the frogs and toads, including Chert, were gathered around, watching with great interest. A number of the other villagers from

Kneecap were there too, though they were pretending not to notice what was going on. One was pruning an already dead tree. Another one, who looked like a witch, was sweeping her already spotless front step.

"What's going on?" Twig tapped Pegfoot on the shoulder, partly in the hope that it would stop his off-key singing.

"We're preparin' for battle, obviously, my lad!"

"Oh," said Vile. "Who with?"

"That devil chicken, of course!" Pegfoot rubbed his hands together with glee. "He won't be takin' us unawares again!"

"No, sir, Captain," agreed Porkbelly, stringing up another net. "We'll get 'im this time, for sure!"

Beefstew came over and pulled two clothes pegs out of his apron. He handed them to Vile and Twig. "Here you go! Can't be too prepared, you know!"

"What's this for?" Twig took the peg and looked at it doubtfully. Did he mean for them to try and pin Sumac to the nets?

"Why, for your nose, of course! For the rotten egg stink!" Beefstew grinned, showing off his broken front tooth.

"He will be comin' back, right?" Pegfoot looked hopeful.

"Probl'y so," said Glimfinkle, who looked to be enjoying the spectacle. "Knowin' our luck. He's worse than a bad penny, that rotten wizard." Twig set the gnome down, and Glimfinkle sat on a rock with a good view of everything.

"Well, then, get to work!" Pegfoot pointed unerringly to some buckets of dark black and gooey coal-tar pitch. Next to it were strips of white cloth that looked to have been torn from a mainsail. "String 'em up! We're goin' to trap the rotten beggar!"

Vile and Twig grabbed some supplies and obediently climbed up two nearby ladders. Following the shouted instructions of Unlucky Pete, they carefully tied the strips of cloth from one pole to another and coated them in the sticky pitch. It stunk. When no one was looking, Twig put the peg on his nose. It did help, but also made him talk like he had a bad cold.

* * *

They had just tied up the last of the cloth, when Twig saw a familiar sparkle and shimmer in the air around him. *POP!* Zinnia appeared mid-flap right in front of his nose and performed a pirouette, her tiny arms outstretched like she was in the middle of a dance move.

"*Pixie Poooooosssss*— Aagh!"

She stuck fast to the cloth strips like a fly in the middle of a very sticky, nasty-smelling spider web. She thrashed about but only succeeded in making herself more trapped. Goopy tar was all over her.

"Ha," said Vile. "Looks like it actually works. On annoying pixies, anyway."

For once, Zinnia did not look remotely happy or sparkly. Her face was as red as a tomato. "You! Get me out of here right away if you know what's good for you!"

"Or what?" Vile said before Twig could shush her.

"Or you'll never be getting a Pixie Post delivery from me ever again!"

"*Hmmmmmm. . .*" Vile put a finger to her head like she was considering that. Twig hurried to interrupt before the hag said something that he'd be the one to regret. He'd asked Zinnia once why she was the only pixie that delivered to them any more, even though post came to them from places other than Muckwood, where she was based. It had been because Zinnia was the only one who *would* deliver to them after their first moon on the road, and so all messages went through her. Neither Vile nor Glimfinkle were very good at making friends. Of course, no one ever sent *them* any post anyway.

"I'll get you out!" Twig wiggled his fingers at her and muttered a quick spell, one of the few that Ripplemintz had taught him. It was very good for unsticking things, including wizards. Twig had used it to detangle Ripplemintz's long beard from a gloppy potion more than once.

Zinnia came free and flew away, almost getting stuck again until Twig carefully plucked her out of the air by pinching a corner of her dress. Her tiny face was still very red. Twig put her on his shoulder, and she smoothed out her dress and patted down her hair, brushing off the now dried bits of tar.

"I'll, uh, climb down where it's safer," he said.

"You do that," she said warningly, no trace of sparkle or lilt.

He did, Vile following him down and stifling a giggle. "So, Zinnia," he said brightly before Vile could say anything else rude, "what message do you have for me today?"

Zinnia perked up a bit and went right into Witch Wormwood mode. It was a little disturbing how well she could do it.

"Dear Twig,

Good luck with your investigation. Just so you know, Prince Igneous isn't the only one who has gone missing. King Mervyn's oldest boy, Huxley, disappeared about a month ago after babbling some nonsense about finding true love. Considering he's got the personality of a half-rotted turnip and is only interested in boar hunting, I'm guessing he'd had a curse of some kind put on him. Word is, there's missing royalty from nearly all the kingdoms. Do with that what you will, but do try and stay out

189

of trouble.

Sincerely yours, Witch Wormwood"

Zinnia gave him a sharp look exactly like Witch Wormwood would have. Twig felt a small shiver go down his spine.

"Oooh, did you get some Pixie Post, then?" Unlucky Pete walked up, wiping the pitch off his hands and on to his shirt. It looked like it wasn't the first time he'd done that. "We haven't had any post here in ages! 'Course, most people move here to get away from that."

"I've got another *mess-age*! For Twig Thicket, *wizard extra-or-dinaire!*" Now that she had more of an audience, Zinnia was back to trilling at full throttle.

She twisted around once in the air and took on a blocky shape that Twig was all too familiar with, but she started shouting before he could stop her.

"TWIG THICKET! WHY HAVEN'T YOU ANSWERED ME BACK YET? BACON THE PIG'S GONE LAME AGAIN AND YOU NEED TO FIX HIM UP JUST LIKE NEW IF YOU KNOW

WHAT'S GOOD FOR YOU. I TALKED TO THE
KING, TOOK ME BANGING ON THE CASTLE
DOOR FOR HOURS, BUT—"

Zinnia stopped to take a breath. Twig stuffed a sugar cube in her mouth again. He was starting to wonder if she always took a strategic breath in the middle of his mum's messages on purpose to get extra sweets.

"Huh," said Unlucky Pete. "Now's I remember why we don't have a Pixie Post box here on Bone End." He stuck a finger in his ear and wiggled it around and then wandered off.

Zinnia swallowed down the sugar cube with an equally sugary smile. "I've got one more for you," she said and twirled herself around again in the air. She pushed some imaginary spectacles up her nose and squinted her eyes.

"Dearest Twig,
  I am just writing to warn you that your mother may be a teensy tiny bit upset with you. Also, she's had a word with King Mervyn about you working

for him. I, of course, have told him I know nothing about anything, which is mostly true, so I'm sure he believed me.

I do hope you are well wherever you are. By the by, if you happen to see Kudzu, can you please tell him he owes me for fifteen broken containment bottles and my entire collection of robes. He sent me one of those dratted beauty bombs of his and I'm still picking flower petals out of my beard and trying to remove a rose bush from the middle of my wardrobe. I had no idea they were so hardy. Or thorny.

Best of luck, Ripplemintz"

"You could have given me his message first, you know," Twig said to Zinnia, as she took off the pretend spectacles.

"Don't blame the messenger," she said primly and opened her mouth wide for another sugar cube. He popped one in.

"Any return message?"

"Ask Witch Wormwood if she can send a barrel of dragons' tears," said Vile.

"It'll be extra for delivery of that!" said Zinnia.

"OK, OK," said Twig, and gave her a long message for Witch Wormwood explaining the current situation. He handed the pixie five sugar cubes and promised her more upon her return.

"Pixie Post awwwwaaaayyyy!" She made the sugar cubes disappear and *poofed* away in a shower of pixie dust. Twig sneezed.

"Do you think that witch actually has dragons' tears?" asked Chert hopefully, scrambling over to them with Glimfinkle hitching a ride on his back and looking inordinately pleased about it.

"Maybe," said Vile. "Mostly, I just want to see that silly pixie try to cart a barrel of it here."

"Aye," chuckled the gnome. "Me too! Should've asked for a few more things!"

IN WHICH THERE
ISN'T A KNIGHT

They had almost finished all of Pegfoot's planned renovations by late afternoon, including a catapult loaded with a smelly assortment of stuff, which they'd attached to the top of the Shin and Bone with Twig's magic and a whole lot of coal-tar pitch. Twig almost hoped Sumac *would* make an appearance so they could get some use out of all the work they had put in. Of course, it was a small price to pay for a decent roof over their heads.

He'd even made up a few batches of glass bottles that he'd filled with various spells: odour neutralizers that could turn rotten egg stink into the smell of spice cake, small but potent fireballs, and dung bombs, just because.

Vile had taken some of the glass containers and made them into witch bottles, which had confused Twig, as it didn't sound at all like hag magic. But it turned out they were for repelling curses, which she thought was prudent as Sumac's nan had been one of the best hags in all the kingdoms before he had stolen her magic.

Twig didn't really understand the witch bottles; some of them had only a single castor bean in them and others looked completely empty, though Vile assured him they were not. Hags were a mystery in more ways than one. He kind of wanted to see how they worked. On the other hand, he was hoping to never see the boil-covered chicken again.

They were just putting the last touches on bushels of half-rotted fruit and veg for loading into the catapult, when they heard the clip-clop of a horse approaching.

"A guest! Quick, boys, to your stations!" Pegfoot, who had been napping in a hammock made out of a fishing net, sprang to his feet. Porkbelly slid down a ladder and stationed himself smartly by the door, while Unlucky Pete dived in an open window to disappear inside the inn. They heard a crash and a shouted "I'm OK, Captain!"

"Oh, it's Sir Thinly of Bragmore," said Twig, recognizing the horse. There weren't many horses that thin. It matched its owner.

Pegfoot deflated a bit. "Ach, another lovesick puppy, then."

"Nah," said Vile. "Well, sort of. But only one woman's got a spell on him, and she's on the horse with him."

"Oh, another hag?"

"Er, no," said Twig. "Her name's Quinsy and we met her on our way across the Seven Sisters. . ."

"Surely you don't mean the siren?" Porkbelly took a hard look at the approaching riders and then frantically fumbled in his pockets after he got a good look at Quinsy. He dumped a few things out until he found something squishy that looked a bit like the bread they'd had at breakfast and stuffed some in his ears.

"Here, Captain, don't move, it's the siren. Let me put something in your ears."

"Oh, no," said Pegfoot. "Just tie me up!" He had a strange smile on his face. "I haven't heard a siren song since I lost me leg."

"I thought it was the devil whale that got your leg," said Vile.

"Same difference," said the pirate.

"It's OK," said Twig loudly, stopping Porkbelly from stuffing the bread in Pegfoot's ears, "she's promised to stop, uh, you know, luring people to their doom."

"Huh," said Porkbelly. He didn't take the bread out of his ears.

"Well met!" Sir Thinly rode up on his horse, which looked even more gaunt than before somehow. There wasn't much to eat on the Seven Sisters. Sir Thinly dismounted and then carefully helped Quinsy down off the horse. She gave a surprisingly graceful curtsy to them. "It's been a long time," she said to Pegfoot.

"Aye," he said, still with the strange smile on his face. Twig wondered what she had sung of to him. Epic battles in the middle of the Deep Sea? Piles of plunder?

197

"Sorry about the leg," she said. She laid a hand on Sir Thinly's arm. "My dear Roddy says I should apologize whenever possible." She smiled, which was probably meant to be a friendly smile, but still somehow seemed a bit terrifying. Maybe it was how white her teeth looked against her red, red lips. Or the fact that they were slightly sharper teeth than it seemed like they should be. "Of course, I'm afraid it isn't possible to apologize to most of the men I've sung to. . ."

"Er, right," said Twig. He cleared his throat. "So, uh, what brings you two here?"

It was Sir Thinly's turn to clear his throat and blush. "Well, as you know, I've long wanted to be a fisherman. And now that I've found my dear Quinsy, I intend to make that dream a reality and give up my knighthood. But" – he leaned forward and dropped his voice to a whisper – "I must confess that Quinsy's former, er, home isn't terribly . . . comfortable."

"It's a pile of rocks," said Vile.

"Yes, well, be that as it may, we thought perhaps we might settle in Kneecap. I understand it to be a place where everyone is welcome, no matter what they might have done before or who they are." He looked hopefully at Pegfoot and Porkbelly and around again at the neighbours, who were busy pretending not to watch what was going on.

The pirates fell about laughing, even Unlucky Pete from inside the inn, who stuck his head out the window.

"Ah, lad, you've got it all wrong," said Pegfoot. "We're not welcoming at all. Bone End is a miserable place full o' rocks and sand and little else. But what we *are* is a place where people mind their own business." The witch sweeping her very clean step *humphed* and kept sweeping, but with a small smile on her face. "So's if you want to stay, we'll not stop you. As long as there's no luring any locals to certain doom. We keep to ourselves here."

"Oh, I don't do that any more," said Quinsy sweetly. "Though if you ever do want to hear a song, just for fun..."

"Yeah, no," said Porkbelly quickly, before Pegfoot could say anything.

* * *

Sir Thinly and Quinsy took a room at the Shin and Bone to stay in until they could build themselves a house and joined everyone for an early supper. Sir Thinly gave Beefstew an entire bag full of fish that he'd caught, possibly with the help of Quinsy. It wasn't just men that she could lure with her voice. Of course, she wasn't used to eating fish cooked, but no one else wanted to eat them raw. Beefstew made a bunch of fish pies.

"Have you made any progress in finding Prince Igneous?" asked Sir Thinly.

"Possibly," said Twig, and filled him in about Nasty and the Kraken's Toothpick and how he had been chased out the window of the tower. He'd been arguing about it all day with Vile while they worked, and they hadn't yet figured out how they were going to get back in to get the prince out. He'd tried and tried to get her to agree to just remove the curse from Nasty, but Vile was still flatly refusing. She was as stubborn as his mum and kept muttering about getting back at

Nasty for all her years of abuse.

He did understand her anger, even if he didn't agree with it. After all, he had brothers and sisters too, and they were nearly as annoying as Nasty, though a lot less dangerous. The only thing his brother Badger could do was fart on command. But she still didn't seem to understand that it wasn't just about an epic sisterly squabble. Other people were getting hurt too.

"So, then, you think the prince is probably in the tower, but you don't think you can sneak back in?" Sir Thinly asked.

"Yep," said Twig glumly.

"His exit was rather dramatical," said Glimfinkle. "I don't think they'll soon forget it!" The gnome flapped his arms and squawked like a seagull while crossing his eyes.

"And only princes and knights and the like are allowed inside?"

"Seems like," said Twig. He looked down at himself. He'd changed his clothes back to how they normally were. Somehow, he felt even scrawnier and more knobbly kneed than before.

"Well," said Sir Thinly, "I don't have need of my armour any more. Perhaps I can teach you how to be a knight well enough to get in?"

Vile snort-laughed and then got a good look at his face. "Oh, you were serious!"

Twig glared at her. She really wasn't helping.

"It could work," said Glimfinkle, "especially if the lad changes his voice with a spell. Or I could ride along with ye and do all the talkin'. What do ye say? I don't sound like I'm wet behind the ears."

"I guess it's worth a shot," said Twig.

"And if that doesn't work, I say we go in with a bunch of your fireballs and dung bombs," said Vile, shoving a big bite of fish pie into her mouth.

"That I'd pay good money to see," said Pegfoot. "If I could see, that is."

18

IN WHICH THERE IS AN ANGRY CHICKEN

Sir Thinly was helping Twig try on the armour after dinner when Beaky, who had eaten all the fish that Beefstew hadn't used and retired to the roof for a rest, let out a tremendous bellow that made the walls shake. The bell in the village rang out – *clang, clang, clang.*

"It's finally time!" Pegfoot shouted. "The devil bird is back! Men, to your stations!"

Porkbelly and Unlucky Pete, who had been watching the knightly fashion show, rushed past Twig to take up their positions on the roof of the Shin and Bone. They were manning the catapult and fishing nets. Beefstew ran outside, carrying another basket of rubbish topped with the leftover fish bones from dinner. Vile followed behind him, her fingers already twisting into a complex hex.

Twig clanked after her, holding up the visor of Sir Thinly's too-large helmet so he could see. He had only put on a few pieces of the armour, including the greaves on his right leg, the gorget collar around his neck and the undershirt worn beneath the breastplate. He felt like a one-legged knight trying to run a race, but there wasn't time to either take it off or put the rest on, not if Sumac was already outside.

Pegfoot grabbed a spear by the front door and ran full tilt outside, whooping loudly as he went. Glimfinkle grabbed Beefstew's ladle and held it over him like an umbrella as he followed behind, much more slowly.

Sumac the chicken seemed to almost be glowing with a fiendish red light in the dusk. He hovered ungracefully in the air, flapping his bedraggled wings and screeching in a very un-chicken-like way. You didn't have to speak bird to understand that he wasn't happy. A round of rotten eggs came raining down, splatting on the ground with a *sploosh*. The stink was everywhere at once. Twig's stomach twisted and he grabbed one of his anti-stink bottles.

"Glimfinkle, what's he saying?" asked Twig.

The gnome listened for a minute. "He says he'll keep comin' after us until the wee hag changes him back and there's nothin' ye can do about it." As if to punctuate the threat, a rotten egg landed right on top of Sir Thinly's helm and dripped down the slits in the visor. Twig gagged.

"Vile," he gasped out, "maybe you should—"

"You must be kidding," said Vile. "He *literally* tried to kill you, Twig. Do you think he'd actually just potter off into the sunset and be a nice little wizard if I uncursed him?" She spun around, releasing the hex she'd been working on in one smooth motion up into the air towards Sumac.

Vile's hex hurtled through the air, invisible to the naked eye, but Sumac was no normal chicken. He wasn't even a normal wizard. His magic had borrowed a lot from his nan, and she had been one of the best hags the world had ever seen, outside of the Hornwort family. He saw the hex coming and dodged it with an impressive aerial display of very non-chicken-y agility.

"Blast!" said Vile, and began working on another complex curse immediately. Twig could tell it wasn't any kind of run-of-the-mill boils or itchy foot. The more she looked like she was doing an interpretive dance, the stronger the curse. He *almost* pitied Sumac. Almost. He had to admit that she was probably right about the horrible wizard. Even Ripplemintz and Witch Wormwood had agreed it was safer for everyone in the kingdoms to leave him as a chicken.

Twig threw one of his no-stink bottles at the ground and took a deep cleansing breath as the sulphurous stink was replaced by the smell of baked goods. The reprieve didn't last long, but it wasn't Sumac's fault. Up on the roof of the Shin and Bone, Porkbelly and Unlucky Pete launched a catapult full of rotten veg and rubbish. Unlike a cannon ball, it was a loosely packed gloppy mess, and as soon as it was launched, it came apart and rained down upon everything. On the positive side, some fishbones and potato peels scored a direct hit on Sumac. But everyone else was also hit.

Other villagers were coming out of their houses to see what was going on, many of them holding their own makeshift weapons. The witch that had been sweeping her step came out with her broom held high and a war cry that made Twig wonder if she was half banshee.

The appearance of more people didn't seem to give Sumac pause. He flew in circles, dropping rotten eggs in an ever-widening pattern. *Splat! Sploosh!*

Pegfoot, who was poking his spear energetically into the air, took an egg directly to the nose. Another hit Glimfinkle's ladle so that it was dripping green goo. Porkbelly launched another catapult full of rubbish. This one was full of leftover fish stew and, apparently, some of Unlucky Pete's dirty socks. There was hardly a clear spot of ground anywhere you looked.

Sir Thinly, looking strangely pale and even thinner out of his armour, picked apple peel out of his hair. He'd followed Twig outside. "What in all the kingdoms is happening?" With everything that had been going on, no one had bothered explaining to him why there

was a catapult on the roof of the inn, and he hadn't thought to ask because he hadn't wanted to be rude. For all he knew, that's how it always was in Kneecap.

"Evil wizard transformed into a chicken," said Glimfinkle, from under his dripping ladle. He had taken up position by the fire to keep the torches lit.

"Ah," said Sir Thinly. "You must mean the wizard Sumac. Fitting, I suppose. I had hoped to never see him again." He grabbed up a fire lance from the stockpile, and a torch to light it with, and took aim.

A fire lance wasn't exactly a lance at all. It looked more like a quarterstaff, but with a hollowed-out pole as the base. It was loaded with black powder and pebbles. A wax-covered bit of string stuck out the top as a fuse.

Ripplemintz had used black powder once or twice in his experiments, like the time he'd blown a new window in the tower not exactly on purpose. Twig couldn't help himself. He saw what Sir Thinly was doing and ran. Vile, still getting ready to cast her next hex, was dancing dangerously near the area. Twig tackled her to the ground right as the fire lance went off with a Ka-*BOOM*!

Three things happened, pretty much at exactly the same time.

Sir Thinly proved that he was at least as good a knight as he was a potential fisherman. The fire lance discharged and the pebbles – plus one very unfortunate snail that had accidentally been loaded into it as well – exploded into the air directly towards Sumac the chicken like a target had been painted on his feathered and boil-covered back.

Sumac, distracted by the fishbones and potato peels, was in the middle of a loop the loop manoeuvre to try and dislodge them from his feathers. He was more upside down than right side up when he caught sight of the knight aiming at him. He squawked and inadvertently let loose a barrage of fiery hard-boiled eggs. But since he was upside down, it propelled him with a spurt towards the ground instead of into the air.

Vile's half-formed hex flew off her fingertips and into the air. Sumac, trailing flaming hard-boiled eggs behind him, barrelled directly into it. There was a *WHOMP* and a *FIZZLE*. Feathers exploded in every direction, punctuated by the *ping! ping! ping!* of pebbles (and snail) as the fire lance's ammunition flew through the air where the chicken had been. Something fell from the sky and landed with a thud behind the wood pile.

"What was that?" asked Twig. "Is he ... is Sumac ... gone?" He felt a bit sick to his stomach. "Did you blow him up?"

Vile shoved him away. "Did *I* blow him up? Shouldn't you be asking Sir Thinly that?" She stood up and brushed herself off. "*I* was only casting my granny's speciality on the rotten bird."

"So, more boils?"

"No, Hornwort's Hasty Hairloss. He's got enough boils already." She helped Twig up. Everyone was standing around in somewhat stunned silence, except for Pegfoot, who was so into the fight that he was still waving his spear in the air as he twirled in a circle and screamed out a sea shanty that had something to do with the high seas and whales. He probably would have kept on, but he stepped on one of the many bits of slippery goo on the ground and he went down. He slid, still singing at the top of his lungs, "O, down his gullet we go, boys! Down the gullet we go!" until he crashed into the wood pile. Logs rolled everywhere. The singing finally stopped and everyone took a breath.

"Captain! Captain!" Beefstew ran to help Pegfoot, but before he got there, the pirate had already sprung to his feet.

"I got 'im!" Pegfoot crowed triumphantly, holding aloft something small and gooseflesh pink and covered in purple-ish boils. A small cluster of very bedraggled feathers stuck straight up from the thing's head, which was held aloft by a skinny neck. A very unhappy snail clung to one naked wing.

"It's . . . Sumac," said Twig.

"See, told you I didn't blow him up," said Vile. "Not that he didn't deserve it."

Sumac, the mostly featherless, boil-covered chicken, tried to flap his wings to take off, but without feathers, all he managed to do was flop around in Pegfoot's grasp.

"Quick, boys, get me to the cage!"

That was enough to get things moving again.

Beefstew grabbed hold of Pegfoot's elbow and directed him to the cage they'd prepared. It was a makeshift affair, as everything was in Kneecap, with bars made out of whatever had been leftover after attaching all of the coal-tar pitch traps and the catapult to the roof. The two pirates managed to stuff Sumac into the cage, and they slammed the door shut.

"Let that be a warnin' to all devil birds," shouted Pegfoot. "Don't be messin' with Bone End!"

Sumac's angry squawks were drowned out in the rousing cheer that followed from everyone in the town.

IN WHICH THERE IS NOT A
DAMSEL IN DISTRESS

"How do I look?" asked Twig. After cleaning the rotten egg and other mess from the day before off the armour, Sir Thinly had managed to put all of the pieces on Twig. There were a lot, especially on the arms and legs. Twig tried to do a twirl, but only managed a clanking half circle.

"Like a cooking pot with legs," said Vile.

"I think you look very knightly," said Sir Thinly diplomatically.

"It doesn't suit you," said Quinsy, "but I was never a fan of armour. It's hard on the teeth."

"Right," said Twig. It made his skin crawl just the tiniest bit every time the siren said something like that, but he knew she was trying her best. She'd even promised Pegfoot that she'd sing a sea shanty with him sometime and she'd taught Beefstew her favourite jellyfish recipe.

Twig had used his magic to make the armour a bit lighter and shorter. But even though it fit him now, he didn't feel at all like a real knight. He barely felt like a real wizard, even with all his magical power.

"Ye best let me do the talkin'," said Glimfinkle. "Ye don't sound the least bit like a knight, present company excepted. No offence." The gnome nodded at Sir Thinly, who looked a great deal more like the fisherman that he wanted to be than the knight he had been, now that he was wearing some of Unlucky Pete's old clothes.

"None taken," said Sir Thinly mildly. He'd even begun to grow a scraggly beard, which somehow managed to make him look even thinner.

"I don't know if that's a great idea," said Twig. The gnome was a lot better at insulting people than getting them to agree to things. "I could try and talk like a grown-up."

"No, he's right," said Vile.

Twig and Glimfinkle both whipped around in surprise. "What?" and "Wot?" they said in unison. Twig nearly fell over but managed to catch himself just in time by grabbing the back of a chair. Moving in armour wasn't the same as moving in wizard robes. Everything was a little bit slower. And clunkier.

"Every knight I've ever heard, other than Sir Thinly, was a right know-it-all," said Vile. "Glimfinkle's great at that. And besides, Twig, you're eleven and you sound it."

"Nearly twelve!" he squeaked, which didn't help his case. He cleared his throat and tried again, speaking as deeply as he could. "I can do it."

"Ye didn't managed to pull off bein' impressive last time," said Glimfinkle. "Besides, what if they recognize your voice?"

"Yeah," said Vile. "Look, all you need to do is bluff your way in there, find Prince Igneous, and throw this on him." She held out a special curse-removal witch bottle she had made that morning. "This'll make him snap out of that wonky love attraction spell Nasty put on that letter. It wasn't super strong, so this should do it, even though I didn't have any dragons' tears. Nasty's a lot better at turning people into frogs than making them fall in love."

Twig took the bottle. It contained a strange murky liquid that looked like it had come from the depths of Rot Bog, with some unidentifiable things floating in it. He hoped they were plants. "What about all the other princes and knights in the tower?"

Vile waved her hand. "I don't have enough for everyone, and we're only being paid to bring back Prince Igneous, right?"

Twig frowned. He didn't like leaving all the rest under Nasty's spell. Some of them certainly hadn't seemed very nice and they *had* chased him out of the tower, but still. It wasn't their fault they'd been cursed. "I'm not here just to collect a reward," he finally said. "Wouldn't I be nearly as bad as Sumac if I just left the rest of them to be turned into frogs or stuck in that tower?"

Vile sighed. "Look, I'll see what I can do. But in the meantime, just go get Prince Igneous, OK? One thing at a time. We have to start somewhere, and we might as well start with the one we've been sent to rescue." She picked up Glimfinkle and held him out to Twig. "Don't forget your grumpy old man voice."

"Hey! Watch who yer callin' old! I'm only in my late one hundreds! Practically a babe in arms!"

* * *

Beaky, having eaten up everything remotely edible that had been thrown at Sumac the day before, including potato peels, fish bones, and probably even Sumac's discarded feathers, was big enough to carry Twig even wearing the armour. He flew them up to the Kraken's Toothpick in no time. Too fast, in fact. Twig didn't feel prepared at all.

He dismounted clumsily behind the same large rock where they had first encountered Sir Moreton and plucked Glimfinkle from his perch atop Beaky's head.

"You ready?"

"Yeh, yeh, just remember to let me do all the talkin' 'cause I don't fancy takin' a tumble out the window, OK? Especially not when yer wearin' a suit of armour."

Twig opened the visor on the helm and poked Glimfinkle in. There was just room for the gnome to squeeze in, though it put him awfully close to Twig's nose.

"When was the last time you had a bath, Glimfinkle?"

"Not that long ago," said the gnome. "When was the last time ye brushed yer teeth, eh?"

"This morning!"

"Whatever ye say. Let's get a move on, I don't wanna be in here all day."

It wasn't easy to see where he was going while wearing the helmet. There were two narrow slits in front of his eyes, but since it had been made for

Sir Thinly, they didn't line up exactly for Twig. It also wasn't all that easy to breathe, even without the gnome smell. The bottom of the helm had round holes punched in a pattern to allow in air and to let you talk, but they weren't very big at all. That was just as well, since otherwise people would be able to catch a glimpse of the gnome's tiny red-clad bottom or his pointy hat.

Even so, Twig managed to make it to the door of the Kraken's Toothpick without falling and only stubbed his toe twice. Considering he couldn't see his feet even if he looked down, he thought that was pretty good.

He took a deep breath, regretting it immediately as Glimfinkle had apparently just burped, and knocked before he could change his mind.

The door opened almost at once this time. On the other side was Prince Dash and his brother Prince Bash from Aramore. Twig had an instant flash of guilt. He had accidentally turned their brother into a fly, after all.

"Welcome!" said Prince Dash with a very shiny smile. "I suppose you're here to throw yourself into the ring for Lady Nasturtium's hand?"

"Of course he is," said Prince Bash, very noticeably

without a smile. He grimaced. "Why else would someone be on this dung heap of an island?"

Glimfinkle gave a hearty laugh that made Twig twitch and clank in surprise. "Well met!" said the gnome. "I be but a humble knight come to pledge my . . . my . . ."

"Troth. . ." Twig whispered, suddenly suspecting that it might have been in their best interests to have practised what they were going to say ahead of time.

"Troth? What kind of *ri-diculous*—"

Twig cleared his throat loudly.

"OK, OK, my troth. I be pledging it," said Glimfinkle. "So's are you two whiffle-waffles goin' to let me in or not?"

"Er . . . OK," said Prince Dash. Twig caught a glimpse of the prince's well-manicured hand waving them in and took the opportunity to step inside before Glimfinkle said anything weirder than he already had.

"Ow!" said Prince Bash. "*That* was my toe!"

"Sorry, sorry," said Glimfinkle, not sounding sorry at all. "Hard to see in this blasted thing, ye know." He poked Twig in the nose. Twig bowed his head, hoping that would be enough of an apology. They were really flubbing this up so far.

"Where exactly do you hail from, friend?" Prince Dash sounded very cheerful. Maybe it was because he was the youngest of the brothers. Or he was pretty sure Twig wasn't going to be competition for Nasty's hand.

"Muckwood," said Glimfinkle.

Twig mouthed a silent "Thank goodness". What if the gnome had said Aramore? They'd have been seen through immediately! They *really* should have made a plan first. He needed to find Prince Igneous as soon as possible before they were caught out again.

"Figures," said Prince Bash with a sniff.

Twig felt like he should be insulted, considering Muckwood was where he had been born, but couldn't muster up any indignation. It was a pretty horrible place, all in all.

"Yeh, well—" began Glimfinkle. Twig hurried forward and headed up the stairs as fast as he could go in the armour. *Clunk, creak, clank, creak*. Whatever the gnome had been going to say was lost in the clanking.

"Isn't that Bragmore's insignia, though?" Twig heard

Prince Dash say behind them. Oh no. He clonked hurriedly into the room he'd been in before, where he'd found everyone on his last visit. Was Prince Igneous there this time? He took a look around as well as he could through the narrow eye slits. A bunch of startled princes and knights and the solitary-but-stoic blacksmith stared back at him, but none of them looked like Prince Igneous. He backed out of the room and shut the door. Prince Dash, on the stairs, looked up at him quizzically. Twig waved then darted to the next set of stairs.

"Where ye goin'?" whispered Glimfinkle.

"He wasn't in there," Twig whispered back. "I'm going to try upstairs. I think that's where he must have been last time." *Clank, creak, clonk, creak.* The next floor had two doors. He opened the first one.

Nasty sat at a dressing table with her back to him, putting snarls in her hair. She caught a glimpse of him in the mirror and started to turn around.

"Sorry!" Twig stammered and slammed the door shut.

"See here, now," said Prince Dash, coming up the

stairs after him. "What do you think you're doing barging into a lady's chamber unannounced? We've got rules here, you know!"

"I jus' got lost!" said Glimfinkle loudly. "No harm meant! Didn't see a thing!" He pulled Twig's nose and Twig took the hint. He clanked his way quickly to the next door and hurried through it.

A broad-shouldered man sat on a comfortable chair in front of a fire. He looked up as Twig burst in. He was very solid, with a neck nearly the same size as his head and hands big enough that only one of them was needed to hold the book he was reading. His blue-green eyes were as deep and mysterious as his mother's. Prince Igneous! They had found him!

Twig didn't hesitate. He took Vile's witch bottle out of his pouch, uncorked it, and threw the murky contents directly in the prince's face with a *sploosh*.

20

IN WHICH THE HAG APPEARS

There weren't any sparkles or flashes of light as Vile's curse-removal potion hit the prince square in the face. There was no rush of wind or chimes or anything at all. Also no boils, which was a relief, as Twig had half-expected that to be a side effect of anything Vile made.

"Did it work?" asked Glimfinkle.

"I don't know," said Twig. He turned to Prince Igneous. "Um, sorry about all that. But, uh . . . how are you feeling? Do you feel different, by any chance?"

Before the prince could answer, someone rushed through the door and pushed Twig roughly out of the way. Twig stumbled forward and managed to not fall over by windmilling his arms.

"What did you do!?" It was Nasty. She ran right to Prince Igneous and stuck a shaky finger into the gloop dripping down his face. As for the prince, he mostly looked surprised and damp, but uninjured. She put her finger to the tip of her tongue to taste it, something Twig definitely wouldn't have done. She whirled on him. "It's Ragwort's Remedy! Where did you get this? Who are you?"

"Don't worry, I'm fine," said Prince Igneous. "Just a bit wet, is all." He wiped off some of the goo with one of his big hands and shook it off on to the floor with a *plop*. He had a deep voice like his father, but with a bit of a melodic lilt to it.

Prince Dash appeared in the door. "He's a knight from Muckwood," he said. "Or maybe Bragmore, I'm not sure. He just arrived." He stepped in and took Twig by the arm. "Do you want me to remove him, m'lady?"

"Git yer hands off me!" said Glimfinkle at the same time that Twig said, "Wait!"

Prince Dash dropped his arm and took a quick step

back. "Methinks he's possessed," he said, continuing to inch away. "Perhaps I should get the blacksmith. He's a big fellow."

Nasty grabbed at Twig's helmet and yanked. Twig held tight to the bottom of it and tried to keep it on, but it was hard to hold on to anything wearing the gauntlets. They were like metal mittens. He could feel the helmet slipping from his grasp.

"What's going on here?"

Twig recognized Sir Moreton's pompous voice immediately.

"Help me!" commanded Nasty.

Twig felt another pair of hands grab on to the helm. He couldn't see anything now, as the eye slit was somewhere around his forehead. Glimfinkle was pressed up against his face, clinging to his nose.

"Yer squishin' me, ye rotten hag!" shouted the gnome.

Twig opened his mouth to try a spell, but the gnome grabbed on to his tongue and half-climbed in, trying to keep from being squashed. Twig gagged but tried not to spit him out or bite him. But he lost his grip on the helmet and with a *POP*, Nasty and Sir Moreton managed to pull it off.

The first thing he saw was Nasty's angry but beautiful face, twisted in rage. But the first thing he *heard* was Sir Moreton's terrified shriek, "We pulled off his head!" and then a thump as the knight collapsed on to the feet of a very surprised Prince Dash.

Nasty didn't even seem to notice. "You're Vile's little friends," she hissed. She tossed the helmet on to the ground. It landed on Sir Moreton's stomach, but he had fainted, so he didn't even twitch.

Twig straightened up and squared his shoulders. There was no helping it now. He carefully spat Glimfinkle out into his palm. "Yes, and we're here to save Prince Igneous. His father sent us."

"Me?" said Prince Igneous. "Save me? From what?"

"From the hag's love spell!" said Glimfinkle, pointing a finger at Nasty.

"The Ragwort's Remedy. . ." It suddenly seemed to occur to Nasty exactly what that meant. Her shoulders fell. She still had her back to the prince, but Twig could clearly see from her face that she understood the game was up, at least with Prince Igneous. He wouldn't be under her spell any more.

"Ragwort's what?" asked the prince.

"Hag?" asked Prince Dash, very confused but still polite. "I say, there's no hag here."

"*She's* a hag," said Twig, pointing at Nasty. "And she's bewitched everyone with a love curse. It was on the parchment you all received. She's been lying to you all this time. She's been looking for true love's first kiss as a way to break her own curse."

"Don't be silly," said Prince Dash, laughing.

"*You're* still cursed," said Twig. "But he's not." He pointed to Prince Igneous. "Not any more. Isn't that right, Nasty?"

She growled at him instead of answering and twisted her fingers into a shape Twig was all too familiar with. He pulled out one of Vile's curse-repellent witch bottles, the one with the lone castor bean in it, which he was wearing on a cord around his neck and showed it to her. Twig really wasn't sure it would work, but Nasty took one look at it and deflated. Maybe his dad had been right all those years. Plants *were* good for you.

"Now's we got that settled," said Glimfinkle, "the prince'll be comin' with us, thank you very much."

Prince Igneous, who had listened silently to everything so far, stood up. His head nearly touched the ceiling. Glimfinkle, standing on Twig's palm, looked up and up, trying to keep his eye on him, and fell over flat.

Nasty turned to look at the prince, nervously smoothing out her skirts. It was probably the first time in her entire life she had cared how she appeared to someone else. It suddenly occurred to Twig to wonder why exactly she was so upset and why Prince Igneous had been in a separate room from all the other princes and knights. Was he special somehow?

The prince took a step forward. Pegfoot was right; he did make the furniture shake when he walked. He bent down to look Nasty right in the eye. She stared back, at first reluctantly, and then she raised her chin and looked at him unblinkingly. "Do you want me to go?" he asked her.

She hesitated a moment and then shook her head emphatically no.

"Then I'm not going anywhere," said Prince Igneous. He smiled at Nasty and then turned to Twig and Glimfinkle and looked down at them. "And I'm pretty sure you lot can't make me."

"This is all quite ridiculous," said Prince Dash, prodding at Sir Moreton with his toe. "I am certainly *not* under any kind of love curse. Don't you think I would know if I were?" He sniffed. "Shall we remove this knight and his little talking rat from your presence, m'lady?"

"Rat!?" Glimfinkle scrambled to his feet. "Who're ye callin' a rat? Twig, yer not goin' to let him talk to me that way, are ye?"

Twig wasn't sure what to do. Had Vile's curse removal remedy not worked? "Look," he said to Prince Dash, "you do realize she turned your brother into a frog, right?"

The prince just blinked back at him. "If she did, I'm sure he didn't mind," he said.

"Oh, he minded!" said Glimfinkle. "He was a bloomin' *frog* until Twig here changed him into a fly and—"

232

Twig clapped his hands around the gnome, but it was too late. That, at least, had seemed to sink into Prince Dash's head. He shook his head like he was waking up from a deep sleep.

"You turned my brother into a fly?"

"I, that is—"

"BROTHERS of Aramore! To me!"

"Er. . ." said the gnome, "ye didn't bring yer flyin' cloak by any chance, did ye, Twig?"

A stampede of feet came thundering up the stairs faster than Twig would have thought possible. *Clank, thump, creak, thump, clank*. A horde of princes, led by the princes of Aramore, burst into the room.

"He's a wizard!" yelled Nasty. "Don't let him get a spell off!"

Twig hadn't even begun to *think* of a spell when he was pounced upon in a flurry of ermine-lined cloaks and silken finery. Someone, he wasn't sure who, clapped a hand over his mouth. Another few somebodies picked him up. He tried to twist away, but there were too many of them. Before he knew it, he was being dragged down the stairs. He wasn't even sure where Glimfinkle was until he felt something climbing around under his armour. Somehow, the gnome had managed to find a hole big enough to clamber into.

He wiggled as the gnome scrambled right across his most ticklish rib, but there was nowhere for Twig to go. They had too tight a hold on him and there were too many. He caught flashes of the stairwell and heard the creak of the stairs, then glimpsed the blue sky as they carried him out of the tower.

"Let's pitch him off Knucklebone Cliff!" someone shouted.

Some pulled one way, some pulled another. Twig felt like he was being torn apart. Would he be able to

get a spell out in time once they let him go? What had he cast last time? Hadn't he just said *"Fly"*? Would it work with armour on? But he didn't have his cloak. He tried to think of something else, but his head was in a jumble.

Then he heard the very welcome, deep-throated bellow of an angry boobrie, followed by a fizzle and the BOOM of a fire lance. The mob of princes and knights clattered to a stop. A rain of pebbles fell down upon them, some of them plinging off Twig's borrowed armour.

"Now that we've got your attention," said a voice he was very happy to hear, "kindly put my friend down before I turn you all into chickens. There's something important you all need to listen to."

Someone else cleared their throat, hummed one clear note that floated off into the sky, and then began to sing.

21

IN WHICH THE SIREN SINGS

Quinsy's voice rang out pure and rich and strong. It echoed off of Knucklebone Cliff and carried out over the water. Twig could feel the pull of it immediately, like the notes were worming their way into his ears. Even knowing what she was and what she was doing, he couldn't help himself. When the princes holding him unceremoniously dropped him with a *thunk*, he simply began crawling towards her like he had no control over his body at all. He didn't even notice the gnome's progress up through his armour until Glimfinkle crawled out from under his collar and stuck his whole head into Twig's right ear.

"Wake up, ye bloomin' ninny!"

The gnome's voice was so loud, being all the way in his ear, that the fuzziness in Twig's head cleared just a bit. Enough that he stripped off his gauntlets and clapped his hands over his ears. Glimfinkle ducked just in time to avoid being squashed like a flea.

Even with his hands over his ears, Twig still felt the pull of Quinsy's siren song. It wasn't as strong, but it was still there, like a dream he'd woken up from but couldn't quite recall. He rolled out of the way just in time as Stab the blacksmith nearly ploughed into him on his way to get to the siren. Death by trampling was *not* how he wanted to go.

"Let my ear
Not hear
The siren's song."

It wasn't an elegant spell, but it did the trick. He tentatively took his hands away from his ears. He couldn't hear Quinsy's song at all now, though he could still hear the shuffling footsteps of the steady stream of princes and knights as they tromped towards the siren. They were all enthralled.

He scrambled out of their path and looked back at the tower. Quinsy's song had drawn them all out, every last one of them. Prince Igneous was the last to come through the door. He looked confused. He ran to the closest of the bewitched, which happened to be Sir Moreton, probably because he had just revived from his faint. Prince Igneous grabbed his arm, but Sir Moreton tried to keep walking. The prince was stronger, so Sir Moreton wound up going around in a big circle with the prince at the middle like they were dancing together in a ballroom. Prince Igneous lost his grip as he tried to argue with him, and Sir Moreton continued on his way without a backwards glance.

Prince Igneous took a few more steps and would have grabbed on to the knight again, but Nasty erupted from the tower like a hungry harpy.

"No!" she screamed. "You can't take him!" She gave a running leap and landed right on Prince Igneous's broad back. Much like Vile had once done to him, Twig watched as Nasty smooshed something gloppy into both of the prince's ears so hard that he knew the prince's head would be ringing. He knew the feeling. It wasn't a good one. She must not have known he was a quarter siren and the song didn't affect him.

"You can stop now, Quinsy," said Vile. "I think that's enough." The siren stopped singing. She and Vile were on the back of Sir Thinly's horse. Sir Thinly stood off to the side, holding a still-smoking fire lance. He looked quite proud. Twig wasn't sure if it was because of the shot he'd pulled off or of Quinsy.

"You!" said Nasty from her perch on Prince Igneous's back, her hands still clapped over his ears. "This is all your fault!"

"Because of the Ragwort's Remedy or because I cursed you?" Vile clucked her tongue. "I suppose I could remove it after all. What do you think, Twig? Should I? It's what you wanted."

"Er, OK," said Twig. Had she changed her mind? She'd been so dead set on letting Nasty muddle her own way out before. Had his arguments finally got through to her? He clanked his way to his feet, unsure whether he should head towards Nasty and try to grab on to the prince or whether he should go towards Vile to present a united front. He glanced at Glimfinkle, who was clinging to his shoulder, but the gnome just shrugged.

"Wait!" said Nasty. She slid down Prince Igneous's back and held her hands out to Vile. Twig thought she was going for a hex at first, but she didn't make any weird movements or symbols.

"Oh?" Vile grinned. Twig shivered. She looked too much like her sister when she smiled like that. "So now you *don't* want me to remove the Rapunzel curse from you, then?"

"Rapunzel curse?" Prince Igneous looked from sister to sister, dribbles of something greyish-green coming out of his ears. "What exactly is going on here, Nasturtium?"

Nasty opened her mouth and closed it a few times. She definitely wasn't grinning now. If anything, she looked a bit scared. Twig felt a bit sorry for her. Also annoyed, because who in their right mind basically kidnaps a bunch of princes to try and remove a curse? But sad because maybe, just maybe, she'd found something she didn't know she was looking for in Prince Igneous.

"Excuse me!" Prince Darrold loudly interrupted. "What am I even *doing* here with all this riff-raff?" He sniffed and gave a quick bow to Nasty. "Good day, madam. I would say it's been a pleasure, but somehow, I suspect it hasn't." He stalked off down the trail towards Kneecap. After a moment and a number of confused looks back and forth, most of the rest of the milling crowd of princes and knights began to follow him.

Vile grinned even wider. "Looks like your little love spell is gone." She made a complicated gesture with both hands and then made a motion like she was throwing something invisible at her sister. "And now, so is your curse. You're welcome, sister."

"No!" wailed Nasty and threw her hands over her face. She sank down on to her knees like she'd been melted.

Prince Igneous glared at Vile and put himself between the sisters. He put a large hand on Nasty's shoulder. "Are you OK? Have you been hurt?"

She shook her head but didn't take her hands away

from her face.

"Let me see," he said.

"You can't," she said, her voice muffled. "I'm ugly again."

"Yer back to bein' yer hag-self, ye mean," said Glimfinkle.

"But wasn't that what you wanted?" Twig felt so confused. "Isn't that why you ensorcelled all those princes and knights and whatever? To break your curse?"

"So, you *are* a hag," said Prince Igneous. He crouched down next to her, looking a lot like yet another immovable boulder in the landscape.

"Yes," said Nasty. "Yes, I am." She raised her head, but lowered her hands just enough so that only one eye was revealed. "I'm a Hornwort Hag, as a matter of fact."

"Just like me," said Vile proudly.

Nasty rolled her eye at her sister and then looked back at the prince. "I'm a *very* good hag," she said.

"One of the best," said Vile. "After me, of course. I did beat you at the hag scrap."

Nasty took a deep breath. She dropped her

hands, revealing
her true face. The
too-long twisty, pointy
nose. The thick, bushy
eyebrows peeking out
from under her fringe. The
sharp eyes the murky colour
of toad stew. The crooked,
gap-toothed, thin-lipped mouth. A smattering of
warts and freckles, though far less warts than Twig
remembered. Possibly some of them had been from
competing in hag scraps and had worn off.

But that wasn't the only difference. She didn't look
exactly the same as Twig remembered. For one, she
didn't have the dangerous lopsided grin that made
you fear for your life. Her hair was still clean enough
to be the same brilliant sunset shade as Vile's, though
it had shortened to be a more reasonable length. She
looked softer, somehow. But still, she was definitely a
hag's hag.

"This is me. The real me," said Nasty.

Prince Igneous took a long, silent look at her. "Are

you still the same sweet Nasturtium on the inside?" he finally said.

Glimfinkle made a gagging noise. Twig poked him.

"I'm the same as I ever was," said Nasty, chin high. "I'm still me."

Looking her right in the eye, Prince Igneous leaned in and gave her a gentle kiss, though he had to manoeuvre around her pointy nose. She blinked up at him, surprised. "Then you're still my Nasturtium," he said.

Twig thought for a second that there was a bit of a sparkle in the air, but it was probably his imagination.

"Heh," said Glimfinkle. "Nothin' happened. She's still as ugly as ever."

"Of course," said Vile. "I already broke the curse. She's on her own now."

Prince Igneous helped Nasty to her feet. He shot a glare at the gnome. "She's not ugly at all," he said.

"It *must* be true love," said the gnome. He winked at Twig and leaned in to whisper in his ear. "Or else he's as blind as Pegfoot."

"He's not blind at all, Glimfinkle," said Twig. "And I

think Pegfoot sees more than you do."

* * *

"What changed your mind? And how did you know that would work?" asked Twig as they all made their way back down to Kneecap. Sir Thinly led the way, with Quinsy riding on his horse, the two of them chatting companionably. Prince Igneous and Nasty followed behind, with Twig and Vile taking up the rear. Glimfinkle was still on Twig's shoulder. Vile had wanted to make sure the two lovebirds didn't wander off and so did the gnome. There was a lot of gold riding on it, as Glimfinkle had already reminded them. Twice.

"Well, I thought about what you said about it not being their fault, the silly lot," said Vile, "and you're right – but don't quote me on that and I won't be saying it ever again. And I still don't exactly get why that's *our* problem. Anyway, I got talking with Quinsy," she continued, "and there's really *three* ways to break a hag curse. One, have the hag that cast it remove it. Two, make up a batch of Extra Strength Ragwort's Remedy using dragons' tears. Or three, cast an even bigger spell on 'em to bewitch 'em."

"I'm very good at bewitching," called back Quinsy.

"Yes," said Sir Thinly, "yes, you are." He looked even more proud, if that was possible.

The few princes and knights that hadn't already made their way down to Kneecap straggled along behind them, including Stab the blacksmith. He seemed the most cheerful of the lot, maybe because he had the least amount of distance to go to return home.

"But what about removing the Rapunzel curse. How did you know that Prince Igneous would still love her?" Twig whispered.

"I didn't," said Vile, looking at him like he'd grown another head. "I'm a hag, not an oracle, you know."

"But—" He stuttered to a stop, not sure how to even ask what he was wondering. "But why did you remove it then?" Had she done it because she thought the prince would leave Nasty?

"To be honest, I hadn't planned on removing the curse until I saw them together. I've never seen Nasty that upset, not even when Uncle Wolfbane fell into a bottomless well and we never heard from him again.

She *is* my sister. I think … she might actually have learned something from all this after all." Vile grinned. "Besides, if someone doesn't love you, warts and all, then they don't really love you at all, right? She should know what she's getting into and so should he. I mean, look at us! We get along just fine and we're about as different as honey milk and toad slime!"

"That's … actually kind of beautiful, Vile." He couldn't argue with what she'd said. It was even sort of nice. For Vile, anyway. Though he hoped she meant he was like the honey milk and not the slime.

"Not to interrupt this wee love fest, but what're we gonna do with the two of them?" asked Glimfinkle. He nodded his head at the prince and Nasty walking hand in hand. "We still gotta get 'im home to Rockpool."

"Oh, he's going," said Vile. "One way – or one hex – or another."

22

IN WHICH
PROMISES ARE MADE

Kneecap was a scene of utter confusion. The returning princes and knights had descended upon the Shin and Bone, demanding everything from rooms (and insisting what was available wasn't nice enough) to food (but sending back what they were served for not being suitably luxurious) and drink (of which there wasn't enough, seeing as how it was the most customers at one time that the inn had ever known). The other residents in the town had even been pressed into service. Prince Darrold had already met the business end of the local witch's broom and was in a corner nursing a probably well-deserved bump on his head.

As they came into town led by Quinsy atop the horse, the ex-pirates were lugging out a large pot of stew and trying, not very successfully, to get everyone to form an orderly queue.

Nasty, head held high, and unapologetically holding hands with Prince Igneous, didn't even flinch as all eyes turned to her. Some of the former victims of her love spell looked like they were angry and wanted to say something, but they took one look at the bulk of Prince Igneous next to her and suddenly were very interested in the stew. The rest seemed too embarrassed to even do that much.

But then there was a sudden chorus of croaks and squeaks and chirps. A flood of frogs and toads spilled out from the Shin and Bone. They hopped and squiggled and leapt towards Nasty like a rolling green wave. As they reached her, the ones with sticky feet jumped on her and stuck fast. The others did their best to cling on, attaching themselves as well as they could to her dress and boots and even to her face. She tried to pluck them off, but that just made them climb more frantically until she was covered from head to toe. All you could see of her was her pointy nose.

"Get them off me!" Nasty yelled.

"I think they like you," said Vile. She had a smile on her face like she had thought something like this might happen.

"Are they still under the love spell?" asked Twig.

"I'm no wee hag, but even I can tell *that*," said Glimfinkle.

"Proximity matters," said Vile. "Why do you think she threw 'em out of the tower?"

Prince Igneous did his best, but the frogs were determined. For every one he plucked off, another would jump up to take its place. Everyone else just stood and watched with varying levels of amusement, except for Pegfoot, who was busy eating his bowl of stew and having a conversation with himself because no one was listening to him.

"Why don't you just remove the curse or hex or spell or whatever it is?" asked Twig as he watched Nasty grumpily flicking frogs off.

"I don't *remove* curses," she said, "I *cast* them."

"And how's that workin' out for ye?" Glimfinkle asked. He looked pleased.

Vile jumped the queue and took a bowl of stew from Porkbelly and sat on a log. "I could watch this all day," she said with relish.

Prince Ash of Aramore approached, carrying a jar containing an agitated fly buzzing around in circles. Twig grabbed his own bowl of stew and ducked down to sit beside Vile. He kept his head lowered.

"I demand that you un-curse my brother," Prince Ash said to Nasty, holding up the jar. Twig sank further down. "Or the Kingdom of Aramore will be *very put out*. I recognize you now, you foul hag. How could you resort to such trickery when my generous kingdom houses you?"

Nasty made a rude noise. "I'm a hag," she said, shrugging off a couple of frogs. "What even is that in the jar?" she asked. "I don't do bugs."

"Er, Vile," said Twig in a whisper, "does Nasty really never ever remove curses?"

"Nope," said Vile. "She's like Granny Scab that way."

"Can Quinsy sing the frogs and, er, the fly back to normal?" Vile *had* said there were three ways to remove a hag's curse, right? To have the hag remove it, the Extra Strength Ragwort's Remedy, or for a bigger spell to be cast on them.

"Nope," said Vile again. "Sirens only charm human men. They don't transform 'em."

He bent even closer to her ear, hoping Prince Ash, who was still arguing with Nasty, who was still trying to scrape the frogs off, wouldn't hear. "So why didn't my transformation spell work then?"

"Hmmm," said Vile, savouring a bite of stew while she thought. "Maybe because it didn't count as a bigger spell? It's probably a question for Ripplemintz, you know, or Witch Wormwood. All I know is that wizard magic doesn't compete well with hag work." She tilted her head at him, mimicking his whisper. "What're you so worried about it for, anyway? It's not like anyone but the frogs know you were the one who changed whatshisname into a fly, and *they're* not talking."

"*AAAAaaaaaaaggghhhhhhrrrrmmmm,*" cried a small voice. Chert Boulderwort, the frog with a beard, had just been tossed in their general direction. Vile caught him before he fell into her bowl of stew.

"And what are you two sitting over here talking about?" asked Chert, his head momentarily clear of the love spell, perhaps from hurtling through the air.

"Nothing!" said Twig. He shot Vile a look.

"I do hope you're going to do something about this situation with your sister—" Chert made the mistake of turning his bulbous eyes upon Nasty and immediately went all starry-eyed. "O, Nasturtium!" He cried and leapt out of Vile's hand towards her sister.

"We've got to do something," said Twig. "Besides the fact that they didn't deserve to be turned into toads—"

"Are you sure about that?" asked Vile. "Look at that prince over there. He seems pretty awful, if you ask me." She gestured to Prince Darrold, who had stolen someone's portion of bread and was being whacked over the head by the local witch's broom.

"Vile!" Sometimes he really didn't understand hags. And here she'd just admitted he was right not half an hour earlier, but he knew better than to bring that up. She'd deny it for sure. "Awful is one thing, but being turned into a frog is another thing entirely!"

"OK, OK," she said. "Don't get your robes in a twist. Knowing Nasty, she probably didn't have a good reason anyway. But *I* can't make her do anything and I don't have the dragons' tears to make up the Extra Strength Ragwort's Remedy. So, unless you know a *really* unhappy dragon, our best bet is to drag Prince Igneous off to Rockpool and let them deal with the frogs after we get the reward money."

"I'm fer that!" said Glimfinkle, popping up on to Twig's knee like he'd been attracted by the very mention of gold.

Twig didn't like it. He didn't like it at all. It was his fault, after all, that Prince Cash was currently a fly. That was certainly worse than being a frog. How long did magically transformed flies even live? What if Aramore figured out it was his fault their youngest prince was a bug? They were the most powerful of all the kingdoms. It was one thing to be on the bad side of Muckwood, but another thing entirely to be an enemy of Aramore.

He felt the sparkly sizzle of Zinnia's arrival before he saw or heard the pixie. She was being cautious this time; instead of popping up in mid-flight, she went *POP!* directly on to his shoulder. He jumped and spilled half of his stew.

"I really wish you wouldn't do that," he said, trying to focus on her. She was so close, all he could really make out was her hair piled high atop her tiny head.

"Pixie *Pooooosssssttttt!*" she sang out.

"That's really not necessary either," said Twig, sticking a finger in his ear to try and clear the ringing. "We know that's why you're here, Zinnia." Then he had a thought. "Wait! Did Witch Wormwood send the dragons' tears?" They were saved!

Zinnia sniffed and flew off to hover in front of him, making sure to avoid any flying frogs, as Prince Igneous was still trying to get them off Nasty. She put her hands on her hips, looking extremely put out.

"Dear Twig,

*Why in the kingdoms would I have an entire
barrel of dragons' tears? They're even rarer than
hen's teeth, as Vile should well know. I've sent along
the bottle that I had. I know that's not enough, but
I've sent out a call to some witches via Pixie Post.
Not sure if they'll help or not, but good luck to you
either way.*

Sincerely yours, Witch Wormwood

*P.S. I may or may not have said that the winner
of the last Euphonium would owe them a favour if
they coughed up the goods."*

Zinnia plopped a small bottle full of a thick liquid that glittered and glistened into his lap. Twig grabbed it before it could fall and break. He turned to Vile. "How many can you cure with this much?"

Vile took the bottle and sloshed it back and forth. "Eh, maybe two or three, if they're Chert's size."

"We're gonna need a whole lot more," said Twig. "But, I guess we'll do what we can—"

"If you've not got a return message, I've got to run," interrupted Zinnia. "Witch Hazel is calling."

Twig waved her off. "Yeah, thanks, Zinnia. You were really helpful."

The pixie beamed broadly at him and *POP!* she was gone.

"I guess we should start with the fly," said Vile. "And Chert, since it's honestly a bit disturbing to have a talking toad yelling at us all the time. I'll get started on the remedy. Beefstew has most of what I need in his kitchen."

"And Chert works for the king," said Glimfinkle. "Mayhap he could put in a good word fer us and we could talk that reward up a bit."

Twig was going to tell Glimfinkle off for only ever thinking about gold, even though he knew it was useless, but there was a sudden *POP!* right by his head.

"Did you forget something, Zinnia?" he asked, turning towards the sound.

"Zinnia!" A sharp-faced male pixie shook a finger in his face. "Do I look like a Zinnia to you?"

"Er, sorry," said Twig. "Not at all."

"*Humph*, me name's Frizwick Morningdew and don't you forget it. Now, which one of you is Twig?"

"That's me," said Twig meekly.

Frizwick cleared his throat grandly and struck a pose, hand on his hip in mid-air.

"*Greetings, Twig Thicket,*

Witch Wormwood told me of your need. Enclosed please find a thimbleful of dragons' tears. I shall be in contact later regarding payment. Cheers.

Sincerely, Witch Hollyhock"

Frizwick pulled out a thimble brimming with the shining liquid. "Where d'you want it?" he asked.

Before Twig could answer, there was another *POP!* and another and another. *POP! POP!* Three more pixies, two carrying thimbles and one with a small potion bottle full of dragons' tears, were flitting about his head, jostling for space.

"A Pixie Post parcel for Twig Thicket from Witch Ruellia!" chirped a tiny pixie with pigtails.

A stout one almost flew into his nose. "Me first!

Delivery for Twig Thicket, Euphonium Winner, from Witch Motherwort!"

"No, me!" said the third, a pixie dressed all in rose petals, "Package for" – she managed to look slightly apologetic – "some upstart young wizard with a silly name from Witch Crowberry."

"I'll, uh, go get a spare barrel from Beefstew," said Vile as a dozen more pixies *POPPED* into view, all holding thimbles and bottlecaps and even one carefully balancing a saucer filled with dragons' tears.

Twig gulped. He was going to owe a lot of favours to a lot of witches after this.

IN WHICH THERE ARE NO
MORE FROGS

An hour or so later, they had collected an entire barrel of the stuff and managed to send all the pixies on their way with IOUs to all the witches. Twig had lost count towards the end, but he was sure they would remind him when payment was due. Witches were like that.

The dragons' tears smelled like seawater with an undercurrent of soot to Twig, but there was something weirdly oily about the liquid. It looked like it was moving, even when it wasn't.

Vile grabbed some lemons, jars of herbs and other things from Beefstew's kitchen shelves and unceremoniously dumped it all into the barrel, along with a pouch of something from her own bag. She stirred the concoction with a poker from the fireplace, while reciting some seemingly random words and doing a bit of a jig as she danced around it, arms and legs akimbo. The mixture bubbled and fizzed, even though it wasn't anywhere near the fire.

The frogs were still trying to swarm Nasty, and Prince Igneous was still trying, very unsuccessfully, to get them off her. Nasty, however, seemed resigned. She'd managed to grab a lukewarm bowl of stew and was trying to eat it, even though a tiny tree frog was swimming around in the bowl.

Twig plucked it out, just in case she accidentally ate it. Besides, it was someone's son. And it might be a prince from a kingdom as powerful as Aramore. He held out the wee frog to Vile.

"Is the Ragwort's Remedy ready?" He hoped the frogs wouldn't have to drink it. It didn't look edible.

"Nearly," she said. "Just needs one more thing to make it extra *extra* strength." She walked over to her sister. "Nasty," she said.

"What?" snapped her sister.

"Nothing," said Vile, quickly reaching over and pulling out a single strand of Nasty's hair. "Just wanted you to know this was me." She dropped the hair into the barrel as she said a few more words over it: *"Spittle! Twinge! Splat!"* The liquid immediately stopped bubbling and fizzing and turned a particularly glowy shade of green.

Twig *really* hoped the frogs and toads didn't have to drink it. It looked like the kind of thing that would turn you *into* a toad, not transform you out of one.

Vile grabbed the ladle that Glimfinkle had used as an umbrella during the battle with Sumac. She plopped the tiny tree frog into it and then dunked it in the barrel to scoop up a ladleful. She just managed to pull it out before the tiny frog began growing in every direction in a confusion of limbs and green goo and exclamations of surprise.

"I say!" said a confused prince from Dunmire a moment later, patting himself down as if to make sure every bit of him was still there. "I do have the most horrible taste in my mouth!"

Prince Igneous had been watching Vile with both mistrust and interest, especially when she plucked the strand of Nasty's hair. But after he saw what had happened to the tree frog, he began plucking handfuls of the frogs off Nasty and tossing them directly into the barrel.

This was not the best idea he had ever had.

By the time the tenth or eleventh frog had been pitched in (Prince Igneous could move pretty quickly when he wanted to), the first couple of transformed princes were exploding out of the barrel full-sized and sputtering. A couple of the knights even came out wearing their armour, now tinted green by the Ragwort's Remedy. But Prince Igneous kept right on tossing them in. Nasty, for her part, just kept eating her stew.

The prince was tossing the last of the frogs and

toads on to the top of the frothing barrel when the entire thing exploded. Princes and knights and globs of green goop went everywhere. Luckily, some of it wound up in the jar that Prince Ash was still holding and plopped right on to the fly sitting dejectedly on a rotten apple core at the bottom. Soon, Prince Ash was juggling his brother instead of a jar, surrounded by shards of broken glass.

The courtyard in front of the Shin and Bone looked like a family of trolls had exploded.

"What's that smell?" asked Pegfoot, nose in the air. "There's a stench of some wicked haggin' going on."

Twig was going to magic away the mess, but Glimfinkle stopped him before he did. "Ye best watch who yer doin' yer magic in front of," said the gnome, nodding his head at the assortment of green goop-covered royalty from all over the kingdoms, and in particular at Prince Huxley of Muckwood. The prince looked a great deal like his father, King Mervyn. He had just as many sharp angles.

"Ah, good thinking," said Twig. He really didn't want it getting back to Muckwood exactly how much power he had left. So he picked up a broom and got to work. Vile made everyone else pitch in too, threatening to curse anyone who wasn't helping. Given that a great deal of the crowd had very recently been hopping and croaking, that proved an efficient threat.

Even Zinnia, who had returned with some dragons' tears from Witch Hazel, helped, though her idea of assistance was to randomly sprinkle pixie dust on everyone as they worked and to trill out "Well done, *yoooooooouuuu!*" periodically. Soon, everyone was feeling very happy and a bit light on their feet. Pixie dust had that effect on people. Even Nasty had her toes tapping and a whistle on her lips, though she looked annoyed every time she clicked her heels. The gaps in her teeth made her particularly good at whistling. Prince Igneous, though, was perhaps the happiest person there.

"You're all invited to the wedding!" he announced grandly, perhaps forgetting that nearly everyone there who wasn't a resident of Kneecap had just been released from Nasty's love spell or frogmification.

Everyone cheered. At least, everyone that had been

hit with pixie dust.

"Show me to the Pixie Post box! I must send word to my father! This will be the biggest celebration the kingdoms have ever seen!" There were more cheers and a small smattering of jeers from the princes of Bragmore and Aramore. Bragmore had long had a rivalry with Rockpool, and Aramore firmly believed it was in charge of anything biggest or best in the kingdoms. To be fair, Aramore was usually correct.

"We haven't got one," said Unlucky Pete. Even though he had been inside the inn when the barrel exploded, he was still covered in goo, but it seemed to have done him some good. He hadn't stubbed his toe once.

"Nonsense!" sang out Zinnia, leaving behind a sparkling trail of pixie dust as she flew over to the prince. She was practically glowing. Twig wondered if pixie dust also had an effect on pixies. Maybe that was why she was nearly always so cheerful. "I, Zinnia Coreopsis Borage, can take your message!"

"Excellent! Tell my father to expect us tomorrow and to prepare for the wedding of the century!"

Zinnia *POPPED* away before Twig could add anything to the message, like how they had managed to free the prince from the love spell (though not from being in love) and had transformed Rockpool's court wizard back into a person and de-frogged a whole parcel of princes.

* * *

The next morning dawned earlier than it had any right to, mostly because Sumac, still locked in his cage, began crowing before the sun actually came up. This made Twig inordinately glad that Pegfoot had asked them to leave the featherless, boil-covered chicken at the Shin and Bone. The old pirate thought Sumac might draw visitors to Kneecap, similar to the famous six-legged purple sheep that lived in Titchington. Twig wasn't sure about this, but it was better than taking the foul fowl with them.

Princes and knights were snoring everywhere, sleeping wherever they had fallen once the pixie dust had worn off. Everyone had stayed the night on Bone End, not wanting to chance crossing the Seven Sisters in the dark. Even with Sumac's noise, it took Porkbelly throwing buckets of water on some of them before every last one was roused.

By the time the sun was all the way up, everyone was fed and on their way, having eaten everything the pirates had in their larder. Since Beaky hadn't had his fill given the competition, he was only big enough for Glimfinkle to ride, so Twig and Vile walked along with the rest. They stuck as close to Prince Igneous as possible, just in case, but also to keep an eye on Nasty. Twig didn't quite trust her, even if she did seem to only have eyes for the prince.

The princes and knights that had managed to find their horses soon outdistanced the rest. By afternoon, the line of people stretched all the way from Rockpool to the middle of the Seven Sisters. Sir Thinly and Quinsy had even agreed to go on ahead, if only so Quinsy could ask her sisters to let everyone pass unmolested.

Twig and Vile, along with Nasty and Prince Igneous, were somewhere in the middle of the pack. The prince and hag kept cooing at each other and giggling as they walked, never letting go of each other's hands. They looked happy, if a bit greenish. The Ragwort's Remedy was exceptionally sticky.

They weren't the only ones. Twig looked down at himself and at Vile. Many strange things had happened in the last few days and a lot of it had been messy. Other than his cape, which still fluttered proudly after him and currently looked like the sunniest of sunny skies, he looked like he'd been dragged through the mud, dunked in a vat of rotten things, and then dragged back through and then baked. Though he did smell like vanilla and cinnamon from the un-stink bottles. Vile didn't look much better, not that she probably cared.

But they couldn't go to a wedding looking like this. Not even Nasty's. He checked to make sure Prince Huxley of Muckwood wasn't anywhere nearby and no one was paying attention.

> "Wind and sun,
> Sand and sea,
> Make some wedding
> Clothes for me."

A shower of sparkles fell down upon him like a gentle spring rain and then whirled around Vile as well. He closed his eyes, while she let out a surprised yelp. It was a nice spell, this one. It felt like the warm sun was shining down upon him while a sea breeze blew. It tickled a bit. As it finished, it almost sounded like the waves slowly receding away at low tide.

He opened his eyes, anxious to see what the spell had done. But the first thing he saw was Vile, and he was stunned into silence. The spell had changed her too; she was the cleanest he'd probably ever seen her, even after a bath. But it wasn't just that. She was dressed in an elaborate white gown. A delicate sea-foam-like veil sat atop her red curls.

He looked down at himself. He was dressed head to toe in a matching white-on-white suit of sorts. It was even fancier than Vile's dress. The trousers were like silk and tucked into boots that could only be described as gleaming like silver and sunlight. Pearly buttons decorated his tunic.

He swallowed and looked at Vile again. Her face had turned the bright red of strawberry jam.

"Er, sorry..." he said. "This isn't exactly what I meant to do..." He was pretty sure his face was about the same colour as hers. He certainly felt very, very warm. Was the sun warmer here by the Deep Sea?

She ripped the veil off her head and took a deep breath. "Let's just not ever mention this again, OK?" She stomped off, her back stiff.

He decided it would be best for everyone if he didn't tell her she looked pretty. He quickly cast another spell to add some colour to their clothes so they didn't look like a bride and groom and hurried to catch up.

IN WHICH THERE IS TRUE LOVE

Zinnia, perhaps over-fuelled by pixie dust, had gone above and beyond. She hadn't just informed the king and queen of Rockpool of the impending nuptials and the rescue of princes and knights from across the kingdom. No, she'd also told a fair few of her fellow pixies, who'd each told a handful more, who'd then delivered the message throughout the kingdoms. There *might* have been an ogre somewhere deep in the Eternal Forest that didn't know, but it was doubtful. Pixies were dreadful gossips.

When Twig's little group, including Prince Igneous and Nasty, arrived in Rockpool, the entire city was out to greet them. But it wasn't just the residents of Rockpool. Anyone within a reasonable distance was there as well – they'd come on horseback, in wagons, on foot and, in the case of Pumice Pummelstone, the court wizard of Aramore, on a wheeled contraption powered by wind. Pumice's arrival actually eclipsed their own until people noticed Prince Igneous holding hands with Nasty.

"Is *that* his bride?" Twig heard someone ask.

"Is that a *hag*?" added a shopkeeper.

"Not just a hag. That's a *Hornwort* hag," said a page, possibly from Aramore, as they were wearing the colours.

Nasty merely held her head up higher and clomped ahead, holding tight to Prince Igneous's hand. She had changed into troll-hide walking boots for the journey, so it was very effective stomping indeed.

Prince Igneous didn't even notice the stares or the whispers or the occasional wagging finger. He was busy pointing out places of interest to Nasty, like the shop that had his favourite kind of watermelon pickle or the tree he had once fallen out of when he was seven years old.

"Do you think they're going to be OK?" Twig whispered to Vile.

She answered him with another question. "Do you think Nasty cares what people think?"

"Well, no, but..." He wasn't sure how to say it. People could be cruel and Nasty wasn't exactly what most people thought of when they imagined a princess. After all, wasn't Prince Igneous the oldest of King Jasper's children? That meant she'd probably be queen of Rockpool one day! He'd never heard of a hag being a queen before. They mostly kept themselves to themselves or to their hag huts. Though, the current queen of Rockpool *was* half siren.

"I wouldn't worry," said a lilting voice suddenly. Twig jumped and turned to see the oracle had joined them as they walked. She looked just as he remembered her: barefoot, with her long, simple gown all dusty along the bottom where it dragged the ground. She smiled at him in that infuriatingly knowing way she had.

"What are you doing here?" he asked.

"I'm here for the wedding, of course," she said. "I've been here two days already. You took a little longer than I thought you would."

"You knew?" Twig stopped walking until Vile whacked him on the back to get him started again.

The oracle raised her eyebrows at him.

"Right," said Twig. Of course she knew. She *was* the oracle.

"I never miss a wedding," said the oracle. "That's where you get the best cake, you know."

"Ooooh," said Vile and picked up the pace. "I didn't think about the cake! I've never had wedding cake before! I wonder what flavour it will be?"

"So, *you* think they're going to be OK?" he asked the oracle, waving at the prince and Nasty.

"It looks like True Love to me," she said. You could hear the capital letters. "How about you?"

He took a really good long look at the couple as they ambled down the street oblivious to everyone else. Even though Nasty was stomping and pointedly ignoring the crowd, there was a smile on her face the likes of which he had never seen on her before. It wasn't cunning or shiver-inducing or threatening at all. It was a good smile. It was a perfect match for the one on Prince Igneous's face, though it seemed much more natural on him.

Twig rubbed his eyes. Was it his imagination or did the two of them almost have a glow about them? It wasn't the sun bathing them in soft yellow light. It was coming from them and the way they smiled at each other. "They're beautiful!" he blurted out and then blushed. "I mean, yes, it looks like True Love to me too."

"I knew you'd find it," said the oracle.

He blinked at her. She was smiling that smile again.

"Find what?" asked Vile.

"Beauty," said Twig. "The prophecy. We found beauty where there was none, and so has Prince Igneous. And Nasty too, in her own way. She's found her own beauty by finding it in someone else. And, you know, we even found it in each other, I think. When we stop arguing long enough."

The oracle patted his shoulder. "I did tell you, you know. Love is beautiful, in all its shapes and sizes and forms."

Vile sighed. "Have you ever thought about just telling people things directly instead of making them guess what you mean with your little prophecies? You could have saved us a lot of trouble."

It was the oracle's turn to blink, though it most likely wasn't in surprise. "What would be the fun in that?" she asked, but she didn't wait for an answer. She turned on her heel and disappeared into the crowd.

"I *really* wish she'd stop doing that," said Vile.

"I'm sure she knows that," said Twig. "That's probably why she does it."

Vile punched him lightly on the shoulder. "You do know we're not going to stop arguing, right?"

* * *

They were all ushered directly into the throne room

as soon as they arrived at the castle. King Jasper and Queen Coral were waiting, along with the young twins, Prince Flint and Princess Shale. Twig wasn't sure how old they were, but they were definitely younger than he was. The difference was that they looked very royal, standing at attention next to their parents, all dressed in their finery. Chert Boulderwort, who had managed to find his horse and had beaten them back to Rockpool, stood off to the side. It might have been Twig's imagination, but he still looked a little like a frog about the mouth.

Glimfinkle and Beaky had already arrived as well and made themselves at home. Beaky, currently about the size of two magpies smooshed together, was perched on the shoulder of a page who was standing as still as possible and periodically feeding bites of fruit to him very carefully. Glimfinkle was sat in his saddle on Beaky's back and thoroughly enjoying a grape.

"About time ye got here," said the gnome as they came in, though he didn't look particularly upset. From his rounded belly, it was obvious that it wasn't his first grape. "I've told the king and queen all about wot we did!"

Servants bustled everywhere, carrying loads of flowers and platters of food. The hall was half-decorated with bunting and streamers. A plush carpet had been carried in, so their footsteps were muffled.

Queen Coral stood as Prince Igneous entered, dragging Nasty along behind him. For the first time, the hag was hanging back.

"Mother!"

"Son!"

The prince rushed forward, pulling Nasty along with him. He only let go of her to scoop up his mother in a huge, bone-crushing hug. Twig stayed where he was. It seemed like a family moment, even if it wasn't one that he could imagine having himself. His mother wasn't the kind of mother you hugged.

But Glimfinkle didn't have any such qualms. "Y'see, yer majesty, I told ye we'd get the prince back to Rockpool, all safe and sound!"

That got the prince's attention. "I was always perfectly safe," he said, letting his mother go. "I was with my Nasturtium." He took Nasty's hand again and pulled her forward. The king and queen got their first proper look at their son's prospective bride.

"She *is* a hag!" gasped Prince Flint. His sister kicked him.

"As I warned you, your majesty," said Chert Boulderwort.

Twig didn't even have to look at Vile to know that her fingers were itching to cast a curse in the general direction of the wizard. Prince Igneous didn't look well pleased either. Twig cleared his throat and waved an arm in the air before either one of them could do something unpleasant.

"Er, your majesties," he said, not entirely sure what he was going to say next. "As the oracle pointed out to me, um, just a moment ago, sometimes you've got to ... look ... deeper. I mean, OK, Nasty" – Prince Igneous coughed – "*Nasturtium*, that is, well, she's definitely a hag. Like, in every sense of the word."

Nasty shot him a glare that clearly said he wasn't really helping. He tried to ignore it. A point was coming to him. He hoped. "When we first got to Bone End and figured out that it was Nast ... urtium that had kidnapped" – Vile stepped on his toe – "um, *attracted* Prince Igneous, I have to admit that I was really worried."

"Yeh! We knew we had to do somethin' fast!" Now it was Glimfinkle's turn to get a glare directed at him.

"But," said Twig loudly, "True Love *is* beautiful. It doesn't care what you look like or what you are or even if other people might be afraid of you." He looked right in Queen Coral's eyes, those deep blue-green eyes that looked like they'd been dipped right from the middle of the Deep Sea. A siren's eyes. She nodded at him, slowly, as if encouraging him to go on. "And I truly believe that what they've found is True Love and that they deserve all the, um, well wishes that should go with that." He took a deep breath, but couldn't think of anything else to say, so he bowed to the king instead.

After a very long moment that seemed to go on for ever, the king nodded his head once in response. "Well," he said, "it looks like we have a wedding to get on with, then."

25

IN WHICH THERE'S ENTIRELY TOO MUCH BEAUTY

The only weddings Twig had been to before had been for his older brothers. They had been simple affairs attended only by family and held in a small clearing near the Thicket house in the Eternal Forest. The most exciting thing about them had been that they meant someone was moving out of the crowded house and that they got to eat his sister Minnow's not-very-famous lemon brackenberry crumble.

This wedding was different. Guests, invited or not, trickled in throughout the rest of the day. Besides the princes that were already in attendance (having travelled with them from Bone End), more and more royalty arrived. There were family reunions and congratulations and both well and ill wishes (Prince Darrold was still annoyed, though no one was entirely sure what about). Prince Igneous's fairy godmother even showed up, proclaiming that she'd known this day was coming all along, even though the only thing she'd apparently said on the day he was born was that he'd take after his father.

The entire hall was full to bursting when the ceremony finally began. A choir made up of mermaids sang a haunting tune, while a pleasure of pixies formed moving constellations in the air and sprinkled pixie dust over everyone. Glimfinkle, riding upon a man-sized Beaky (he'd eaten a lot of fruit and nearly the poor page's fingers), walked Nasty down the aisle. Beaky stalked proudly to a prominent spot right in front of everyone. No one, not even Prince Darrold, muttered even the tiniest hint of complaint when the witch officiating the wedding asked if there was anyone who had anything to say against the marriage. Twig suspected he knew why Nasty had requested the gnome and bird do the honours.

The happy couple had just exchanged rings when the door at the end of the hall flew open with a blast of perfumed air and a barrage of rose petals. Kudzu of the Spire strode in wearing an entire outfit woven of living flowers and trailing more behind him. "I say, I do hope I'm not too late!"

Twig hadn't seen the half-elf wizard he'd given some of his magic to since the end of the Euphonium. The wizard seemed taller now, but that might have been because of the length of the living cape of greenery that trailed behind him, extended all the way back to the moat. Or maybe it was the sparkling glimmer of fairy lights that danced about his head.

"I bring gifts," Kudzu declared grandly, apparently not at all fussed at having interrupted the ceremony. He pulled a number of embroidered velvet pouches out of his sleeves and held them up. "This will be the grandest, loveliest ceremony since Queen Carnelian of the Spire married, oh so many moons ago!"

"Oh—" said Vile.

"No—" said Twig.

Everything happened very quickly after that. Kudzu immediately tossed the beauty bombs in the air with a flourish and a shower of sparks. One pouch exploded in mid-air into a cloud of . . . clouds. Puffy white and pink clouds, clouds like candyfloss, clouds tinged with gold, like when the sun is hiding behind them. They floated into the air, bouncing off the ceiling.

Another pouch fell to the floor and at first Twig hoped maybe it had been a dud. But then came the exclamations of surprise that rippled out in a wave from where it had fallen. Soon, vines were wiggling like snakes between the rows of guests. Unnaturally large moonflowers bloomed everywhere all at once, bumping people about.

The last pouch, which had been thrown the highest, fell right towards the front of the hall, almost like Kudzu had aimed for the bridal party. It was the largest one and it wiggled as it fell. Right before it would have hit Prince Igneous square in the face, Beaky snapped it – *CLAP* – out of the air.

"What did you do to my gift?" cried Kudzu. "You've spoiled it!"

Twig breathed a sigh of relief. They were saved.

Then Beaky belched.

It was a great big *BRAAAAAAP* of a burp. It echoed. It blew back some of the gathering clouds, twirling them about over the front of the hall so that they spun around like a mini white-and-pink tornado. Some of the clouds turned a stormy grey as they whipped around. There was a crackle like lightning in the air. The hair on Twig's arms stood up.

"*Oh—*" said Twig.

"*No—*" said Vile.

Beaky, already quite large, rapidly expanded to

his full boobrie size. He opened his beak again, but this time it wasn't a burp that came out. Out flew a flutter of brightly coloured butterflies. Then a hover of hummingbirds, darting this way and that. Two of them got stuck in Nasty's hair. Twig hoped that was it, but then an exultation of larks flew out, trilling.

Beaky's beak opened wider. A pandemonium of exotic blue-and-red-feathered parrots from faraway Salamander Spit flew out, squawking and swooping. Like most people in the kingdoms, Twig had never seen one before. Then there came a rumble from Beaky's tummy and his beak opened so wide that it didn't seem like it could possibly go any wider. Out pranced a pride of peacocks, their tails spreading wide as soon as they appeared. They strutted and screamed, sounding almost like crying babies.

Beaky's beak snapped shut.

By this time, most of the guests in attendance had made a break for the exits. There were only two; one that led towards the entrance of the castle and the other to the kitchens. The air was thick with clouds and birds and butterflies. Some of the clouds had begun to rain. The carpet was sodden. The stone was slick. The guests, many dressed just as finely as the peacocks in silks, slipped and slid into each other.

Nasty, her wedding dress dripping with rain and some splotches that looked suspiciously like bird poop, had her hands outstretched towards Kudzu. Prince Igneous, stunned by the spectacle, just stood there like a boulder. The witch performing the ceremony was attempting to hide under her hat, not very successfully, even though it was a very large one. A parrot had landed on it.

Kudzu was wagging a finger at Beaky, as if the mess was all the boobrie's fault. Beaky let out a loud *GRACK* and a *gurgle* like he had a stomach ache. The king and queen were fighting off a particularly unruly cloud that seemed to have a mind of its own. It had settled on top of Queen Coral's crown like it was determined to live there.

It was complete and utter chaos.

Twig had to do something before there was a stampede, or worse. And he didn't even want to think about what "worse" might be. It didn't do to wonder

about that in the kingdoms. He threw his hands up in the air, gathering the magic inside himself and spreading sparkles from his fingertips.

"Save the hag!
Everything –
Back in the bag!"

A few things happened at once. The pouches that had held the clouds and the moonflower seeds shot into the air. The vines that had grown wild shrank just as fast as they had sprouted and flew into the air as tiny, silver moon-shaped seeds again, plinking into the pouch. *Ping, ping, ping!*

The clouds, however, had tripled and quadrupled in size already. Twig couldn't even see the ceiling through them. A sudden warm wind sprang up and blew through the crowded hall, pushing the clouds ahead of them. Twig's cape, made of clouds and sky itself, whipped about but just managed to stay on, held tight by the shell clasp. Everyone's hair blew about and anyone who had started off the ceremony wearing a hat wasn't wearing one any longer. Vile's brilliant red hair stood completely on end, but that might have been because of her hag sense, which was certainly bound to be screaming. Finally, *finally*, the clouds all merged into one great big roiling, tumbling whirlwind spinning against the ceiling.

Then, just when it seemed it might drill through to the next floor above, *WHOOSH*, they were sucked back up by the pouch, as if a giant had drawn in a big breath. For just a second, it felt like all the air had gone out of the room too, but then it all rushed back in.

Meanwhile, something had been rumbling around in Beaky's rather large stomach. Up, down, sideways, back ways. His pitch-black feathers stuck out like he was a very large, very annoyed hedgehog. Everyone near him that hadn't already backed off took the opportunity to get away. Glimfinkle still clung to his neck, looking slightly terrified, but doing his best to pat Beaky in what he probably intended to be a comforting fashion.

"Yer all right, my boy! If ye gotta let out another o' those wicked burps, jus' let it rip! I'm hangin' on!"

Beaky opened his mouth wide and, for a moment, Twig thought he *was* going to let out the monster of all burps. But he'd been so focused on watching everything happening at once that he'd missed that the peacocks had stopped running about and were now all heading back the way they had come. As Beaky's mouth gaped wide, the first of the returning peacocks made a giant leap and dived right in. Then another and another and another. Beaky grew larger and larger as every bird vanished down his gullet.

Then came the parrots, screeching wildly, and the larks, warbling sweetly. The hummingbirds, so quick they were a blur, disappeared so fast it was like they had never been. The butterflies, looking significantly the worse for wear from the whirlwind of clouds, were the last to go.

When the last one was lost to sight, Beaky shut his beak with a *SNAP* that rocked the castle. He shook his ponderous head from side to side, brushing against the ceiling as he did. Glimfinkle could barely be seen clinging to the monstrously ginormous boobrie. Beaky was now the biggest thing that Twig had *ever* seen, easily five times bigger than the ogre that had once tried to eat them in the Eternal Forest. Larger, perhaps, than the whole of Witch Wormwood's cottage. Certainly the largest beast that anyone in Rockpool had ever seen, other than the pirates who had claimed to have come up against the devil whale and lived.

Twig was never sure who screamed and ran first. It might have been Prince Darrold or it might have been, well, anyone. Or everyone. Because scream and run they all did.

Nearly everyone, that is. In just moments, the hall was empty except for Prince Igneous (who had staunchly swooped up Nasty into his arms), the king and queen (who looked surprised but stoic more than anything), Kudzu (who looked annoyed but not at all chagrined), the oracle (who looked bemused and less windblown than anyone else, having hidden behind a wall tapestry through most of the mayhem), Twig (who was trying his very best not to look responsible for anything that had happened), Vile (who had started laughing so hard that she was well on the way to hiccoughs) and, of course, Beaky (who looked, well, *big*) and Glimfinkle (who was clinging on for dear life).

Vile stopped laughing after Twig elbowed her sharply in the side. Twice. "That," she said, "was definitely the best wedding *ever*, except that I didn't get any cake."

"I told Cook to keep the cake in the larder so it would be safe," said the oracle, twirling a bit of her hair around her finger. She was smiling that smile again, even bigger than before. It really was a terribly annoying grin. Not evil or mean, but definitely way too knowing. Which she probably knew.

"Of course you did," said Vile. She was smiling too.

Twig peeked over at Prince Igneous and Nasty and the king and queen. He walked over to Beaky, placing a hand on the boobrie, partly just to make sure he didn't gobble up anything else. He fervently hoped this was a temporary size gain or else they'd need to start a farm just to feed him.

King Jasper was stroking his chin as his gaze took in the state of things. Queen Coral's dark hair, which had always been floaty, was tangled about her in a wild web. She was silent, her eyes even more unknowable than normal.

"What a mess!" Kudzu waved his arms in every direction, taking in the entirety of the hall. It was swampy, with wet carpet, and full of feathers and bird poop and all the hats that had been left behind. Kudzu pulled another pouch out of his sleeve. "I shall fix—"

"No!" said absolutely everyone at once. King Jasper leapt to his feet. He cleared his throat. "That will be quite all right," he said, a little more calmly and kingly. "I've been meaning to have the room redone anyway. Right, dear?" Queen Coral, who had also stood, nodded quickly.

It was Nasty's turn to laugh, but she didn't just laugh. She chortled. She snorted. She howled. That set off Vile too. After a moment, Prince Igneous began to giggle as well. And then so did Queen Coral, delicately, hiding her mouth behind her hand. King Jasper allowed himself just one loud guffaw.

Kudzu threw his hands in the air. "Well, I never!" he said. He gave Twig a very pointed look. "I shall never understand you non-elves. You have no appreciation for beauty or what's right. Why, I've been getting threatening letters from all over the kingdoms about my beauty bombs!"

"Did you ever stop to think that maybe it's not them that's got the wrong end of the stick?" asked Twig. "If there's one thing I've learned, it's that everyone has their own idea of what's beautiful and right and forcing your own version on them is just, well, *wrong*."

Kudzu lowered his hands. "I see, I see," he said. "That could explain things, I suppose. Though everyone *knows* that the elves know best. . ."

Beaky chose that moment to snap his beak with a resounding *CLACK*!

The wizard sighed. Even the fairy lights circling his head dimmed. "It's just that, since you gifted me that extra power, I feel ... *itchy*. What good is it if I can't use my magic to make the kingdoms a better, more beautiful place? But no one seems to appreciate my efforts." His shoulders slumped. "I wish you had never given it to me."

There was a moment of silence, broken only by the sound of water dripping down the walls. "I could ... take it back?" asked Twig.

Kudzu considered for only a minute, twirling a bit of vine around his fingers. "Yes," he said. "You should. It wasn't mine and it doesn't fit. It's been like walking around in another wizard's robes."

Twig nodded, looking once around the room at everyone. Vile nodded back.

"An unexpected gift,
Can a burden be.
So, return to me,
And let Kudzu be carefree."

A whisper of a soft, warm breeze blew through the room, swirled once around Kudzu and then surrounded Twig. It felt a bit like a hug from Witch Wormwood or when he held hands with Vile or even when Glimfinkle patted him on the head. He felt whole again.

Kudzu shook himself with a small smile, bowed low to Twig and then King Jasper, and took his leave without another word.

Twig waited a bit but everyone was holding their tongues as if they had witnessed something momentous, even the gnome. So, he shrugged and cast a simple spell to clean the room. Someone had to get things back to normal. Soon it was, except for the small drift of hats stacked neatly in the corner.

"I thank you," said King Jasper gruffly.

"If yer really grateful," said Glimfinkle from his high-up perch, "I'm sure I could think of a number of glitterin', shiny ways ye could reward us!"

"Glimfinkle!" Twig rolled his eyes. Yep, things were definitely back to normal. Ordinary for them, anyway.

"Wot? Don't ye remember? We were promised our weight in gold as reward for bringin' the prince back, Beaky included." All Twig could see of the gnome was his little red cap as he carefully made his way down Beaky's now very grand neck. "I'm not askin' for anythin' more than wot we was promised!"

Twig and Vile looked at each other, eyes wide. Technically, Glimfinkle was right. They turned to the king, who was stroking his chin again as he stared up and up at the boobrie.

"Well, well," he said. "I am nothing if not a man of my word."

Glimfinkle slid the rest of the way down Beaky and jumped. Twig caught him without even thinking. He was used to the gnome's ways by now.

"I knew stickin' with ye was the right decision, Twig, my boy."

Vile threw her arm around Twig's shoulders. "It's definitely always an adventure," she said. "Usually a messy one."

"Right," said the oracle. "You didn't even need *me* to tell you that."

Twig wanted to sigh, but he also wanted to smile, so that's what he did.

Pixie Pooooost Dee-livery!

Fifteen minutes after the end of the wedding. . .

POP! Zinnia puffed herself up and took a deep breath. Twig braced himself, fearing what was surely to come.

"TWIG THICKET, DO YOU MEAN TO TELL ME THAT YOU GOT INVITED TO SOME FANCY WEDDING AT A CASTLE AND DIDN'T THINK TO GET AN INVITE FOR YOUR FAMILY AND I HAD TO HEAR ABOUT IT SECOND-HAND FROM THAT DREADFUL WIZARD RIPPLEMINTZ? YOU'D BEST HURRY HOME. BACON'S FOOT IS BETTER, NO THANKS TO YOU, BUT HE'S OFF HIS FEED NOW AND YOU NEED TO SORT HIM OUT—"

Twig hastily stuffed two sugar cubes in the pixie's open mouth. He shivered. Messages from his mum were always the worst.

Two days later. . .

POP! Frizwick's sharp nose twitched as he drew himself up to his full height, which wasn't very tall at all. "Got another message for ya," he said.

"Greetings, Twig Thicket,
    Regarding the payment due for the thimbleful of dragons' tears, I will accept either a groat's worth of powdered mermaid scales or, at the very least, eleven cockatrice feathers in good condition and not a feather less.
    Sincerely, Witch Hollyhock"

✳✳✳✳

A day after that. . .

POP! "Pixie *Poooooossssstttttt!*" Zinnia pushed a pair of imaginary glasses up her nose and pulled a long, sad face. She looked quite tired, but Twig wasn't sure if it was her or the message she was delivering.

"Dearest Twig,
    I wouldn't normally ask, but my beard's beginning to fall out from the stress of your mum knocking on my door all times of the day and night. I don't suppose you could possibly visit and sort out her pig, could you? I managed to get some poultice from Witch Wormwood to fix up his leg,

but apparently he's still having trouble of some sort. I am not an expert on pigs. He looks exceptionally well-fed to me.

At any rate, I would also like to show you my latest experiment. I've finally managed to trap a warbler's warble in a time-delay bubble! Works most excellently as an alarm clock.

Best wishes, Ripplemintz"

"P.S. I hope you received the cockatrice feathers in time. Witch Hollyhock, like all witches, isn't to be trifled with. It was the last of my stash, so do please replenish it when you can. Or, if you happen to come upon anything of interest, send it my way!"

"By the way," said Zinnia, taking a sugar cube from his pocket without so much as asking, "I'm going on holiday, so you'll have to do without me for a while. If Cheeseparing comes by, don't blame me." And with that, she POPPED! away.

✾ ✾ ✾ ✾

Exactly one week after the delivery of the dragons' tears. . .

 POP! A pretty little pixie curtseyed apologetically to Twig, before chirpily introducing herself as Cam Happihart, and then completely startled him by snarling out her message.

"*Dear whatever-your-silly-wizard-name-is,*

It's been a week and I've not yet had payment for the dragons' tears. Don't think I won't be complaining to Witch Wormwood about this. I'll accept like for like, if you can get your sorry hands on a sad dragon. Otherwise, send me a half year's supply of salamander spittle. If I don't hear something from you by the end of next week, you'll owe double!

Witch Crowberry of The Edge"

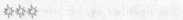

While on the way to Salamander Spit to track down a supply of salamander spittle. . .

POP! POP! Two nearly identical pixies wearing matching maroon and gold jumpers flew right up to Vile and bobbed their heads at her in unison.

"Hi! I'm Tiny!" said the male one.

"And I'm Squishy!" said the female. They almost sounded alike too.

Together, they announced, "And we've got a message for you from the Princes Ash, Cash, and Dash of Aramore!"

"To Mistress Vile of the Hornwort Hags,

Greetings from the brothers of Aramore. If it isn't too much trouble, we were wondering if you would consider stopping by at your earliest convenience. It seems our brother Bash happened upon a stash of something your sister Nasty left behind in her former hag hut on the castle grounds from when she was employed here. He's been transformed into a rather large toad and, to be frank, we're quite tired of catching flies to feed him.

We will, of course, provide compensation for your time.

Thank you kindly, Princes Ash, Cash, and Dash"

�֍ ✿✿✿

Two weeks after the wedding, while on the way to Aramore, robes slightly singed from flaming salamander spittle. . .

Sparkle! POP! With a shower of pixie dust, a pixie dressed completely in sewn-together flower petals slowly pirouetted in front of Twig. "Greetings! I am Sunlily Foxkiss with a message for you." She stopped spinning and took a closer look at Twig. "You *are* the Great Wizard Twig, aren't you?" Not waiting for an answer, she shrugged and struck a dramatic pose:

"Greetings, young Wizard Twig!

I have returned to The Spire and I confess to feeling much relieved to be home and back to my usual self. Tremendous power is a great burden, it seems. Queen Carnelian still wishes to invite you for a visit to show you the wonders of the gateway to the elven realm. Do write back when you get a chance or just stop by! The flowers will let me know you are coming.

Ever faithfully, Wizard Kudzu of the Spire"

"We ain't goin'," said Glimfinkle darkly. "I don't trust elves."

"Yeah," said Vile, "or talking flowers."

✿✿✿

A few days later, leaving Aramore with pockets full of coin, the day after a full moon. . .

POP! A ruddy-faced pixie appeared on Twig's shoulder. "Norbert!" he exclaimed.

"Er, I'm not Norbert," said Twig. "I think you've got your deliveries mixed up."

The pixie cocked his head in confusion. *"I'm Norbert,"* he said. "Post for Twig and Vile!" He leaned in and whispered the message so quietly they could barely hear him.

"Shhhh! Twig and Vile,

This is Wizard Chert. Please do keep this quiet, but are there any known side effects of formerly being a frog? Last night I had the most unpleasant dream of eating flies and this morning I found I'd gobbled up half my pillow. I beseech you to write back at your soonest convenience or visit if you are in the area.

Sincerely, Chert Boulderwort"

Vile let out a giggle. "Oh, that Nasty," she said. "She's tricky. I'll send him some extra Ragwort's Remedy. We really ought to track down a supply of dragons' tears."

✿✿✿

Three weeks later. . .

POP! A smug-faced fairy appeared. "Cheeseparing Crosspatch here with a message from King Mervyn of the Kingdom of Muckwood, care of Simon Pennyroyal, King's Adviser." The self-satisfied look only intensified as he delivered the message.

"*Ahem. Wizard Twig,*

The king has asked me to demand that you speak to your mother about her pig. We understand from Ripplemintz that you might possibly have some reservations regarding employment issues, and he wishes to assure you that he has withdrawn any such ideas if you would just, please, get your mother to stop storming the throne room.

Sincerely, Simon Pennyroyal"

One month later, after the honeymoon. . .

POP! A nervous looking blue-haired pixie Twig had never seen before tapped him timidly on the nose. "Pixie Post from, er . . . someone . . . named . . . Nasty?" She cleared her throat and put her hands on her hips.

"*Yo! Vile and your little wizard friend and that annoying gnome whatshisname,*

We're back from our honeymoon in Rot Bog and my Iggy tells me I'm supposed to write thank yous for wedding gifts.

So, Twig, thanks for whatever it was you did. I'm pretty sure you didn't give me a gift, Vile, so you'd better get on that. Gnomey, don't bother. I don't want to have to thank you for anything.

Smell you later, Nasty"

The pixie blushed. "Sorry about that," she said. "Don't blame the messenger, please!"

***

Two months later, while touring the Falling Mountains looking for a sad dragon. . .

POP! A very titchy pixie popped in and immediately got tangled in Vile's hair. "Oh! Oh, dear!" she said. "Trixie Meanwell here! I've got a message! Oh, my, oh dear! There's a spider in here!"

Twig fished her out, flicking out the spider too. How had Vile not noticed it?!

"Dear Twig,

Glad to hear you've mostly sorted out all the witches you owed and you've gone on holiday in the Falling Mountains. Do watch out for trolls. I've enclosed some slug lollies, just in case. Trolls love them. I would not, however, advise eating any yourself.

Come visit when you get a chance,

Witch Wormwood"

***

A month after that...

POP! A pixie with a mop of messy golden hair grinned at them, giving an exaggerated bow. "Name's Wart! Message for ya from Bone End!"

"Ahoy, there, Twig & Vile & Glimfinkle & Beaky!

Just wanted to thank you all for bunking with us at the Shin & Bone. You were definitely the most excitement we've had in a whale's age. Thought you might be interested to know that Porkbelly's rigged up a contraption to catch any eggs that nasty devil bird lays and Beefstew's figured out a way to pickle 'em to get rid of the stench. He's been selling 'em to hags and making a tidy profit! We've had to add a Pixie Post box to Kneecap, but Wart's not bad as pixies go. He knows not to deliver any loudmouth messages.

So, feel free to visit again anytime, with whatever critters happen to be after ya! We've got the fire lances ready!

Your friend & Pirate in Arms, Pegfoot"

✳ ✳ ✳

After a very quick visit to Muckwood...

POP! Zinnia, looking much refreshed, came in fast, sprinkling pixie dust as she went. "Back from holiday! I've got a *mess-age!* For Twig Thicket, wizard *extra-or-dinaire!*"

"Dearest Twig,

Thank you very much for visiting. I so enjoyed your stories from your latest adventures but especially the quiet it has afforded me. I haven't heard from your mum since you came! Please stop by regularly. Even King Mervyn seems in a better mood.

Yours, Ripplemintz"

❊❊❊❊

Six months after the wedding. . .

POP! Wart, his grin appearing first, materialized in front of them. He had added a miniature sword to his waist and looked quite pirate-y for a pixie. "Post from Bone End!"

"Dear Twig,

Greetings! We wanted to share our good news with you first. Quinsy is going to have a baby! If it's a boy, we're going to name him Twig and if it's a girl, we'd like to name her Vile. I hope that's OK with you, but we thought it fitting as it was the two of you that brought us together.

In other news, we've finished construction of our new house near the Moaning Caves. Quinsy quite likes the sound it makes. She says it reminds her of home and the fishing is quite good in the area.

We both hope you'll visit us after the baby is born, if only to make sure any fairy godmothers that show up aren't troublemakers. You're developing quite a name for yourself!

We even hear the stories here, so I'm sure they would listen to you.

Sincerely, (no longer Sir) Thinly, Fisherman of Bone End"

✦✦✦✦

Sometime later, while exploring deep within the Kingdoms to the north. . .

POP! Zinnia shivered and sneezed, pixie dust puffing up around her. Achoo! "P-pp-pppixie P-pp-pooost!" She glared at Twig. "Message for you, but see if I deliver another one in the snow! It's freezing up here! I am a forest pixie, you know!" She shook off some snowflakes and then put on a very mellow, serene face.

"Hello, Twig,

The Oracle here. I've been trying for many moons to deliver my next prophecy to you, but somehow you have managed to evade me. Of course, I knew you would, but don't think you can escape fate so easily. I will find you when you least expect it, I'm sure. Best wishes to you and Vile and Glimfinkle and watch out for murderous ponies.

Yours, the Oracle"

Pixie Pooooost Awaaayyy!

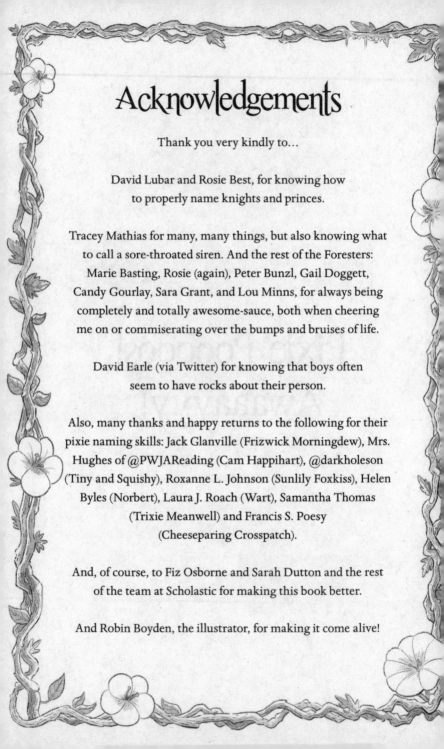

Acknowledgements

Thank you very kindly to...

David Lubar and Rosie Best, for knowing how
to properly name knights and princes.

Tracey Mathias for many, many things, but also knowing what
to call a sore-throated siren. And the rest of the Foresters:
Marie Basting, Rosie (again), Peter Bunzl, Gail Doggett,
Candy Gourlay, Sara Grant, and Lou Minns, for always being
completely and totally awesome-sauce, both when cheering
me on or commiserating over the bumps and bruises of life.

David Earle (via Twitter) for knowing that boys often
seem to have rocks about their person.

Also, many thanks and happy returns to the following for their
pixie naming skills: Jack Glanville (Frizwick Morningdew), Mrs.
Hughes of @PWJAReading (Cam Happihart), @darkholeson
(Tiny and Squishy), Roxanne L. Johnson (Sunlily Foxkiss), Helen
Byles (Norbert), Laura J. Roach (Wart), Samantha Thomas
(Trixie Meanwell) and Francis S. Poesy
(Cheeseparing Crosspatch).

And, of course, to Fiz Osborne and Sarah Dutton and the rest
of the team at Scholastic for making this book better.

And Robin Boyden, the illustrator, for making it come alive!